# Kate took a deep breath. "Now what?" she said.

"That depends," Mike said, tugging mischievously at the sheet.

"I mean, how will this affect us in the office?" she pressed.

"Nicely, I hope. Of course, this'll be hard to manage in the office, what with limited space and those short coffee breaks..." He yanked down the sheet.

Kate snatched it back. "That's not what I meant!" she cried.

Mike's brows knit. "I wasn't planning to paint a scarlet letter on your chest, if that's what you're implying. That's not what last night was all about."

"What *was* last night about?" Kate asked.

"Weren't you there?" he teased, running one finger lightly along the upper plane of her breasts. She felt her nipples peaking in response.

"Yes, but—"

She got no further as he began to kiss her ardently again. "It was about a man and a woman getting to know one another very, very well," he whispered. "That's what last night was about."

Dear Reader:

Last spring marked SECOND CHANCE AT LOVE's second birthday—and we had good reason to celebrate! While romantic fiction has continued to grow, SECOND CHANCE AT LOVE has remained in the forefront as an innovative, top-selling romance series. In ever-increasing numbers you, the readers, continue to buy SECOND CHANCE AT LOVE, which you've come to know as the "butterfly books."

During the past two years we've received thousands of letters expressing your enthusiasm for SECOND CHANCE AT LOVE. In particular, many of you have asked: "What happens to the hero and heroine after they get married?"

As we attempted to answer that question, our thoughts led naturally to an exciting new concept—a line of romances based on married love. We're now proud to announce the creation of this new line, coming to you next month, called TO HAVE AND TO HOLD.

There has never been a series of romances about marriage. As we did with SECOND CHANCE AT LOVE, we're breaking new ground, setting a new precedent. TO HAVE AND TO HOLD romances will be heartwarming, compelling love stories of marriages that remain exciting, adventurous, sensual and, above all, romantic.

We're very enthusiastic about TO HAVE AND TO HOLD, and we hope you will be too. Watch for its arrival next month. We will, of course, continue to publish six SECOND CHANCE AT LOVE romances every month in addition to our new series. We hope you'll read and enjoy them all!

Warm wishes,

*Ellen Edwards*

Ellen Edwards
SECOND CHANCE AT LOVE
The Berkley Publishing Group
200 Madison Avenue
New York, N.Y. 10016

# CLAIMED BY RAPTURE
# MARIE CHARLES

SECOND CHANCE AT LOVE
BOOK

This book is dedicated
with all my love
to Charlie,
who made the world
fade away.

# CHAPTER
## *One*

KATE LONIGAN, BALANCING a drink in her hand, looked directly up and met the clearest, greenest eyes she could have imagined. Their intensity took her breath away. Using all her willpower, she managed to hold the gaze as his eyes continued to regard her thoughtfully. They were set in a deeply tanned male face with fine chiseled features, a high broad brow, and a chin that showed strength. His dark hair curled enticingly about his collar, and the broad shoulders and narrow tapering waist were no disappointment either. Standing several feet away, he seemed about to move to her side. Kate stepped back, allowing him space to approach her on the crowded patio.

Suddenly he turned. Kate watched as he gripped the hand of Albert Baines, the balding, outgoing office manager at Icon Assurance Group, Carson City Branch, and offered his back to her. She reacted as though she'd been doused with cold water. The electrical charge that had sparked between them had been cut off—swiftly, succinctly.

Kate smiled, lifting her glass to her lips. He was, she

**1**

realized, Michael J. Fleming, the troubleshooter selected by the head office in New York to assume the role of temporary office manager and put the flailing Carson City branch back on its feet. He was the only man present with whom she wasn't already well acquainted. And at this party, staged to welcome him, he surely had more important things to do than hobnob with second assistant benefits managers. That was Kate's title, and for a woman of twenty-four it wasn't a bad one to have. But while it gave her a management classification, it certainly didn't put her on a par with Michael Fleming.

Kate didn't wait to see whether he would turn back to her. She set down her empty glass and headed for the buffet table, on which was laid out a far more elaborate repast than was typical for Icon Assurance. There was smoked ham and an array of wax-encased cheeses, also a lobster salad and an assortment of other deli-style dishes. Kate stood, balancing her plate, trying to decide what would be least fattening and most nourishing. She decided on the lobster salad and a thick slice of homebaked wheat bread.

As she turned back to the crowd, her eyes immediately picked Michael Fleming out again. Fortunately he was turned half away from her, and she was now free to scrutinize him without being observed. She took in once again the deep tan, the broad shoulders beneath the white dinner jacket, the narrow hips. He wore no tie, and his light blue shirt was open at the throat—the effect was pleasantly casual for someone in so important a role.

Kate liked to keep abreast of things, and though she didn't normally place great store in gossip, it was hard not to remember all the rumors about the new office manager from New York. At thirty-two Fleming had a reputation as the best crack troubleshooter and organizer in the closed network of the country's fourth largest insurance company. He also had an off-hours reputation as a rogue, an accomplished lover who never lacked for female companionship. Looking at him now, his handsome face animated in conversation with another of the Carson City execs, Kate could see why. He was one of the best-looking men she had ever seen.

Amused, she nibbled at her lobster and bread, noting as her eyes scanned the room that she wasn't the only woman giving Michael Fleming the once-over. Indeed, every female present seemed to have the handsome manager in her line of vision. When he moved slightly to make a gesture or emphasize a point, forty-some pairs of eyes shifted to take in the view. It was quite incredible, really.

Her eyes narrowed slightly as she moved to assess the man in a different light. There was strength in his bearing and power in his very presence. She could see that in addition to being handsome—and charming—this man was tough. Good. Icon Assurance could use a tough captain at the helm. In fact, Fleming had been assigned here because the Carson City branch was in deep trouble. Their accounts were a tangled mess that was threatening to make the entire branch office go under. They had lost two major accounts, and more losses were in the offing if someone didn't get a grip on the bureau. Michael Fleming looked as though he could.

Just then he turned his dark head back in her direction. His green eyes almost burned her as they looked past the crowd and directly into her own. Kate felt suddenly warm, as if he had touched her physically. The contact was stronger than it had been moments before—even though he now stood yards away, in the center of the outdoor courtyard, while Kate still hovered near the buffet tables in the back. The easy smile on his well-defined, sensuous lips seemed meant for her alone. She set down her plate. Her heart fluttered madly. What was wrong with her? She didn't normally react this way. Lord knew, she was no stranger to good-looking men.

As the daughter of Sean Logan, she had known such men all her life. Movie greats had paraded through her house with their picture-perfect faces: her father had entertained them all. There were only one or two directors in Hollywood who had more clout than Sean Logan. And Kate's twin brother Keith had become a film luminary in his own right. Already his romances were reported in *The Crier* and other Hollywood rags—a sure sign that his star was on the rise. Yes, Kate Lonigan knew all about good-looking men.

Yet somehow she—less glamorous by nature—had matured to womanhood unaffected by it all. Until she met Ryan Kilpatrick, that is. Almost literally, he had swept her off her feet, courting her with flowers, expensive dinners, and pledges of love. Yet all the while his motive had been to cull the great director's favor, to further his own stillborn career. In the end both efforts had failed.

Kate's short-lived marriage was the reason she had changed her name, taking on the original family name, direct from Ireland, of Lonigan. She also left her past behind her, making up her mind to pave her own way and be evaluated on her own merits. She didn't want to be known as someone else's daughter or sister. No one at Icon knew anything at all of her background.

She was certainly being evaluated right now, she noted. Michael Fleming's eyes were still fastened on her in what seemed almost like a caress. Instantly she became aware of Gay Ling, another second assistant benefits manager, standing just to her right. Gay had on a slinky mint green designer dress that set off to advantage her smooth, honey-color skin. And other assets. A Eurasian, Gay was atypical of at least her Asian half in that she had a magnificent chest line. The fine fabric and daring cut of her dress took full advantage of that.

Kate waited for the inevitable to happen—for Fleming's gaze to shift to the stunning Eurasian woman. Gay seemed to be waiting for that, too. When it didn't happen, she left Kate's side and, her heels clicking smartly across the patio, was at Fleming's elbow in an instant. Nothing shy about her, Kate thought dryly. When she raised her eyes again, Fleming's dark head was bent over Gay's gleaming dark tresses.

Well, so much for that, thought Kate. Another man gone under. It seemed to be how Gay got away with a minimum of work and a maximum of fun.

Maybe she should take lessons, Kate mused, sitting down on a wicker chair and toying with the remainder of her bread. It certainly beat knocking your head against a wall. She noted her reflection in the sliding glass door leading into the Spanish-style house. It showed her the lithe form of a slim, athletic woman with pale blond hair falling to her shoulders and enough cleavage to tease an appreciative eye, even if there wasn't enough to lose a necklace in.

"Hello."

Kate raised her eyes and looked right up into Michael Fleming's face. He was no longer with Gay, which was surprising. Usually Gay had greater holding power.

He was extending his hand toward her and smiling. Kate juggled her plate and fork, gave up, and put them on the floor, aware that as she did so, her silver-blue dress dipped rather provocatively. When she looked up again, she caught his eyes on the white planes of her breasts. She flushed slightly, then shrugged, reminding herself that after all, it *was* the weekend and this was a party, even if it was a business one. There was no reason not to wear a flattering dress.

She rose and took his hand.

"I'm Mike Fleming," he said. "I hear you're the company agitator." The smile still tugged at his lips. Kate sighed. If you took an action, you got labeled. There was no way around that fact.

Without skipping a beat she responded, "I hear you're the company womanizer."

That stopped him. And then he threw back his head and laughed. Well, at least he wasn't humorless. For some reason she was glad.

"So much for hearsay," he said, gallantly conceding the round to her. His eyes crinkled slightly, making her feel warm all over again. Kate couldn't get over his eyes.

Yes, he was definitely a charmer. She wondered just what else he was beneath his easy voice and manner. She knew he couldn't have risen to his present position by being easygoing. According to what she had heard, he was empowered by the home office to overrule anyone, even Tim Asherton, the Western Region's vice-president. Asherton was used to being a deity unto himself, Kate had observed in her four years at Icon.

Just as she thought of him, Asherton joined them, casting a disapproving eye in her direction with no salutation whatsoever. "I see you've met Kate," Asherton said, his voice cold as he spoke her name.

The smile had never left Mike's lips, and it deepened now. "Yes, I have," he said. It was almost as if they were sharing an intimate moment.

"You will come to realize that she's everything I told you she was," Asherton said, turning Mike toward the back of the patio to introduce him to someone else.

Kate watched for a moment, wondering just how harsh Asherton's description had been. She didn't fool herself for a moment. She was sure he had hit upon all her "unorthodox" qualities, such as the fact that she bent company rules and questioned management policies, even though she was management herself. What Asherton probably didn't tell Mike, she thought, was that hers was the best production unit out of the three in the office, the other two being under Gay and Milt Peters, an owl-eyed man given to theory rather than actual production. But Kate made waves and Asherton didn't like waves, so she could expect no commendations from him. No matter, she could do without his praise. She had her self-respect and the utter loyalty of her unit of forty-two health claims adjusters.

"Wow!" Kate heard one of her female adjusters murmur appreciatively as she stared off in Mike's direction.

"Yes," Kate acknowledged. "And I certainly hope he can get us out of the situation we're in. If we lose one more contract, this office will be closed."

The woman seemed not to hear her as she sighed deeply.

Yes, Kate had to admit, there was plenty to sigh for. And while she would be a fool not to acknowledge Fleming's appeal—and effect on her—her prime concern remained the contracts she administered, the possibility of the office being shut down and policies farmed out to other branches.

Kate liked her work. Insurance wasn't glamorous, but she had had enough of glamour for a long while. Her work gave her a sense of helping people, and while she could readily start again at another company, she didn't particularly want to. She liked the unit and she liked most of the down-to-earth people in the office. It was only when she was up against others in management that she ran into trouble.

But she had promised herself no serious thoughts tonight. This was a party, after all. Her eyes traveled about the area. There was a large fountain in the middle of the courtyard, and a flood of colored lights shone up into the cascading water that descended from a two-tier structure. The entire patio was aglow with party streamers and cream-color lanterns that gave off a warm light. The buffet table was back to the right. A nearby bartender stood behind a makeshift booth that housed a seemingly endless supply of liquor. Kate went off to get herself a second glass of wine. Maybe that would help promote a festive mood.

For the duration of the evening, she mingled with the other people at the party. She even managed to get Albert Baines alone for a moment and say something appropriate about being sorry to see him go. She wasn't really sorry, but it sounded nice. Not that she didn't like Baines. But he was all wrong for his position. Miscast, she thought dryly. He could not control his people, could not make a decision and stick by it, and he vacillated in his office policy, which went from overly lax to strict. Baines had grown more and more miserable as time went on, and his failure had become more and more evident. Morale had fallen sharply in the office. Now he was being transferred.

Mike, Kate observed, had done more for morale by his very appearance than Baines had done in all the years he had tried unsuccessfully to manage the growing office. The next few months were certainly going to be interesting, she mused. She watched people gathering their things. The crowd had already thinned out appreciably. The party was about to break up.

She began to search for Gay, since they had come together in Gay's car. Although Gay wasn't someone Kate usually socialized with, they had a basically compatible working relationship. When Gay had suggested they drive to Baines's house together the night of the party, Kate had agreed.

"Are you looking for someone?"

Kate turned and brushed against Mike Fleming's broad chest. He grinned, as if he enjoyed the momentary contact.

"Yes," she answered, "Gay Ling."

"Gay Ling?" he repeated, as if trying to draw a mental image to go along with the name.

Kate smiled. "The Eurasian woman. In green," she

prompted. "She's my ride home."

Mike made the connection and smiled. "I'm glad to hear that," he told her.

"Why?" Kate asked, slightly puzzled.

"Because that means I can take you home," he said. "Gay won't mind."

Oh, yes, she will, Kate was about to say, but thought better of it.

So he preferred her to Gay! That had to be an office first. Kate was more than flattered—though at the same time cautious. Fleming was, after all, her new boss. It was risky to become involved with the boss. And anyway, he had been forewarned about her: the office agitator. Maybe he thought he could defuse her and win his first office conquest all in one fell swoop. Kate set her chin firmly. Well, he might be in for a surprise. Still, it would be fun waiting him out, watching to see what he had up his sleeve.

"It's nice of you to offer," she told him and turned smartly to lead the way back to the guest room to find her wrap and clutch purse. She was about to throw the diaphanous silver-blue shawl about her shoulders when Mike's hands interfered and he completed the action, slipping the shawl quite purposefully about her bare shoulders. They were alone for a moment in the dimly lit small room, and Kate felt an overwhelming urge to see what it would be like to be kissed by this man.

What a thought about your boss! The words flashed through her mind. The next instant she thought her desire was going to become a reality, but voices drifted toward them, indicating that people were about to enter the room. Suddenly the closeness that had sprung up between them seemed to fade.

He nodded toward the people who came in to collect their belongings before departing and put a guiding hand to the small of Kate's back. She could feel the imprint of his strong fingers through the airy shawl. That'd teach her to wear a backless dress, she thought. But then she hadn't expected to feel this kind of attraction for Michael Fleming.

"We wouldn't want to give them anything to talk about, would we?" Mike said softly, the words almost whispered into her ear.

Had he felt the urge to kiss her, she wondered, looking up into his eyes. Big mistake. Stare at his chin instead, Kate. But that was just as bad. She was tempted to run her fingers along the outline of the marvelous cleft there. Boy, she had better get hold of herself or there really would be something for the office to talk about.

They found Baines and his wife and thanked them for a wonderful evening. Kate made sure word would be left with Gay that she was leaving with someone else. She didn't think it was wise to reveal that the someone was the catch of the evening.

But her good intentions proved useless when they passed Gay on the way to the front door. The woman's mouth dropped open, and the look in her eyes told Kate that any outward sign of friendship had been abandoned for the sake of a larger stake: Michael Fleming.

"Is this yours?" Kate asked Mike, staring down at the open door of the metallic blue Mercedes convertible parked at the curb. The top was down, despite ominous clouds that were beginning to gather in the previously star-filled late-April sky, no doubt presaging one of their sudden, infrequent desert storms. Kate had actually come to look forward to them during her years in this hot desert state.

"I only steal the best," Mike assured her, helping her in.

She laughed as her legs brushed against the soft leather cushions. "Are you always so flippant?" she asked, watching him slip in next to her and start the engine.

"Are you always so outspoken?" he countered, glancing at her.

She knew he was referring to her earlier comment about him being a womanizer. Well, he certainly was living up to his reputation. "I don't back down, if that's what you mean. And I do like honesty—almost better than anything," she admitted.

"Honesty can hurt," Mike observed casually, pulling out of the long, winding driveway.

"Not as much as deceit," Kate said, her voice more serious than it had been as she thought of Ryan. She had paid a high price emotionally for his lies.

"I realize that as the new office manager I'm supposed to know all, but I would appreciate a hint about where you live," Mike said, grinning. "At least the general direction." Apparently he chose to leave her last comment alone.

The somber moment was gone and Kate smiled as she gave directions. She lived only fifteen minutes from the party, but during the short time it took to drive home, the sky produced the promised storm. Feeling two large drops, she glanced up.

"Rain?" Mike asked, his voice none too happy. "Uh-huh," he muttered, answering his own question as a large drop hit the windshield.

Kate turned to him, curious. "Didn't you think it rained in the desert?"

"Well, I was hoping it wouldn't until I got the top fixed," he said. Kate stared at his profile, illuminated by tall lights that lined the streets as they entered the development where she lived. She felt her pulse quicken slightly in the unguarded moment. What a shame he was her boss.

Rousing herself, she realized that they were about to pass her street. "Down here," she said, pointing in time for Mike to make a sharp right into the cul-de-sac.

"The car does turn on a dime, but I usually allow it a quarter," he said dryly. Then he grew more serious as they approached her house, an elaborate two story structure done in stucco with a country-style wood trim extending over the front face. "You live here?"

"Only when I'm not chained to my desk," she told him. A peal of thunder punctuated her words.

"Alone?" he asked, not seeming to hear the noise. He turned to look at her.

"If you're trying to get yourself invited in for a nightcap, it can be arranged," she told him simply.

"That does sound tempting," he agreed, his smile returning. "I guess I was just a little overwhelmed by your house. I didn't know you could afford something like this on a second assistant's salary."

Something in his voice puzzled her, but she shrugged. "You can't," she said honestly. "I have—help," she added with a grin, not really wanting to elaborate at the moment. Her father had refused to let her come to Nevada four years ago, at the tender age of twenty. Finally he had relented, under the condition that she let him buy her a house. Kate had decided her independence could be gained as well in a comfortable house as in a small apartment, so she had accepted his gift.

"A rich relative, really," she clarified more seriously, studying the look in Mike's eyes, not wanting him to get the wrong idea. But she couldn't read his expression. He seemed to be reassessing her in a way she wasn't sure she liked. What was he thinking behind that calculating gaze?

Then his attention went elsewhere. "Oh!" he said as a big drop hit him squarely on the face.

"Besides," she finished, opening the door to the car, "I'm sure you've been told the story of my petition to the home office, requesting a cost-of-living adjustment for everyone across the board. So you must have figured my salary was low. It is, and so are those of the people under me. It's something I'd like to see changed."

A flash of lightning creased the sky, brightly coloring the immediate surroundings. Kate caught Mike looking at her thoughtfully again. He was about to say something when the rain began falling in earnest. Kate ran up to her two-car garage and unlocked the door, pulling it up.

"Drive in here." She motioned, indicating the empty space next to her white Porsche.

Mike made it just in time before the floodgates broke open, attacking the land.

"Whew, that was close," he said, brushing raindrops from his jacket.

"The top really doesn't come up?" she asked, finding it hard to believe that such an expensive car would have such a mundane problem.

"When I hot-wired it, I forgot to check the top." He grinned. "It was a high-pressure situation."

"You didn't really," she said as he came around to join her in the unlit garage, the light from a street lamp providing the only illumination.

He laughed. "No, but when they shipped this cross-country, whoever was handling it did something to the top. Now it refuses to budge. Guess you're stuck with me for the time being—unless you want your new boss to drown," he finished mournfully.

"Heaven forbid," Kate said, fishing out her key and unlocking the door that led from the garage to the house. "At least," she added, flipping on the light as they entered the family room, "not until I find out what your policies are."

"More honesty?" he asked.

She walked over to the bar, setting down her purse and taking out a tall, gilt-edged glass. She nodded in answer. "What's your pleasure?"

His eyes held hers for a moment, sending warm waves dancing across her skin. "You really want to know?" he asked, sitting down on a bar stool.

"To drink," she said, rephrasing her question. "What would you like to drink?"

"Bourbon and Coke," he told her easily.

"Fine, that order I can fill," she said purposefully, and she looked straight into his eyes to see if he caught her meaning. She wasn't sure what was going on here other than her attraction to him, but it was happening much too fast to suit her.

Kate gave him his drink. His fingers brushed against hers as he took it. "You'll find it easier to hold without my fingers on it," she assured him, retracting her hand and pouring herself some wine.

She switched on another light, then sat down on the bar stool next to Mike and sipped slowly, aware that his eyes hadn't left her face. Lord, a woman could get lost in those burning green orbs, she thought, pulling herself back.

"That Porsche in the garage yours?" he asked casually.

"That's what the registration says, although Gladys drives it more than I do," she told him, sliding off the stool to turn on another light. Somehow it made her feel a bit more secure.

"Gladys?" he asked.

"My housekeeper," she explained. "Actually she's more of a chaperon-confidante-friend. She was a gift." Kate laughed, remembering her father's tirade when she told him she was leaving home. Along with the house and the car, he had insisted that she take Gladys along. Gladys had been with the Logan family for years in one capacity or another and had always shown a particular fondness for Kate. The feeling was reciprocated, so Kate had agreed to her father's demand.

"A gift?" Mike echoed. "Correct me if I'm wrong, but didn't the North and South fight a war about that a hundred years or so ago?"

Kate shook her head. "That didn't cover white slavery," she assured him. "Which is what Gladys claims she was sold into."

"And where is Gladys now?"

"In Vegas playing the gaming tables, as is her habit once a month." Kate moved to flip on still another light and turned to find that Mike was right behind her, shadowing her steps.

"Best place for a chaperon-confidante-friend to be," he said, his voice low. "Do you need all these lights?" He switched off the one she had just turned on.

"Only to see," she answered.

"I prefer to feel my way around," he told her meaningfully, his breath touching her temple as he spoke.

"No need for that," she countered. "I've got plenty of flashlights."

"And an answer to everything, I see," he said, amused.

"I try."

The picture window behind them was bathed in an endless sheet of rain. They both looked at it for a moment, then Mike turned toward Kate and said, "Rain is very conducive to love."

"It makes me think of popcorn," she told him brightly, then had to laugh at the look of astonishment on his face.

"Popcorn?" he said incredulously.

She nodded. "When I was young, I was afraid of thunderstorms. To get my mind off that, my older brothers would make popcorn. We'd sit around the fireplace eating it and telling stories while we listened to the beat of the rain on the roof. Now every time it rains I get a craving for popcorn."

"I'm game."

"I bet you are," she muttered as she went into the pantry to find some.

She felt his presence before she even turned around in the small space. As her hand connected with the can of popcorn, she smelled his cologne, which mixed enticingly with the smell of spices. And then she turned and found herself neatly wrapped in his arms.

# CHAPTER
# *Two*

"I HAD NO idea you were so hungry," Kate managed to say, her heart beating harder. The beginnings of mischievousness twinkled in Mike's eyes. "I think we'll get on faster with this if we get out of the pantry," she prompted, the can of popcorn the only barrier between her and this charmingly forward man.

"Oh, I don't know. I like the pantry," he said. She could feel the length of his upper torso pressing teasingly against her, and she knew exactly what he meant.

"Here's the popcorn," she said unnecessarily. "You could help by starting the fire." The rain had turned this April night into a brisk one, and she figured it wouldn't get too warm.

"And how," he asked, his eyes dancing, "do I do that?"

"You start by going to the fireplace—back in the den," she said, nodding in the general direction.

He saluted smartly. "Your word is my command."

"Nice to hear," she said under her breath.

What was she in for here, she wondered as she watched his broad back disappear around the corner to the cozy room at the back of the house. She shook her head, got down the popcorn maker, and hefting it and a large bowl, rejoined him.

She found him sitting comfortably on the flowered sofa that faced the white brick fireplace. There was no light except for the warm glow coming from the fire. Outside, the sound of pouring rain could still be heard. All in all, the situation had the makings of a wonderfully romantic evening—with a man she didn't know at all except by reputation.

Kate put the popcorn maker on the coffee table in front of Mike and plugged it in. She turned back to look at him, a smile tugging at her lips.

"You know, you really are quite different from the run-of-the-mill Icon manager," she told him. The kernels slid into place as she switched on the machine. A whirling noise danced off the silence in the room.

"I take it that's a compliment," he observed.

"It's a judgment," she answered, not wanting to commit herself just yet.

"What were you expecting?" he asked, looking interested as he moved closer to her. Kneeling on the white flokati rug in front of the fireplace, she was suddenly very aware of the vulnerable position she was in. But she didn't move.

"A stuffed shirt," she replied.

Mike grinned, spreading the two sides of his jacket wide, exposing the perfect way his shirt adhered to his firm, flat stomach. "Never been stuffed," he told her playfully.

Kate realized she was staring and blinked her eyes. "How long are you planning to stay?" she wanted to know.

"As long as you'll let me. The rain sounds pretty bad."

She shook her head. "I meant at the office. They said you were here only temporarily." Did that sound as if she wanted him to stay? It did sound a bit eager, didn't it? He was going to think she'd lost her marbles about him... well, maybe she had, just a little.

"I intend to stay as long as it takes to straighten things out," he told her.

"You may have to move to Nevada permanently." She sighed.

"I could think of worse things."

Smooth, Kate thought. Definitely up with the best of them. She found herself smiling at the situation. She was almost buying all this. God, he was attractive in this light—in any light. Probably in the dark as well. Where were her thoughts going? She reminded herself that it would be messy getting involved with the boss. That would be all the Icon officials needed to make her life unbearable. For all she knew, that might be Mike's purpose in singling her out. The thought upset her.

"You have a nice smile," he told her, sliding in closer to her on the floor.

"Five thousand dollars' worth of dental work and braces," she quipped offhandedly.

"They did a good job," he murmured as he lowered his head, cupping the side of her face and raising it toward him.

An initial jolt of electricity zipped through her just before his lips found hers. Then the dimly lit room grew dimmer as she tasted the sweetness of his mouth. She felt his hand glide slowly down the length of her throat and across her shoulder, burning an impression there, causing heat to spring up in its wake as the intensity of his kiss grew, fueled by the response that rose to meet it.

He was taking her breath away. She hadn't thought anyone could do that. Not ever again. She'd let it happen once, and that had been a mistake.

Yet what Mike was making happen to her was delicious and wonderful, a total rebirth—even if it was a little frightening.

Kate wedged her hands up against his chest just as he was beginning to slide down the thin straps of her evening dress. She used her wrists to halt the slipping material before her breasts were completely exposed.

"I think the popcorn's ready," she murmured, seizing on this diversion.

Mike brushed his bronzed fingers softly across her cheek. "Are you involved with anyone?" he asked.

Kate hoped it wasn't too obvious that she was drawing in a deep breath in order to steady her voice. "Do you always ask these questions of your subordinates?" she asked lightly, pouring the popcorn into the large clear bowl. She rose. "We need salt," she said, heading for the kitchen.

"Only those who intrigue me," he called out after her. "And you could never be anyone's subordinate."

Kate stopped to get a glass of water. She felt the sudden need to have the coolness cascade through her veins. When she heard his remark, she set the glass down. "Very good," she said glibly, coming back into the den. "That line will get you a very good response when properly applied."

"Is it being properly applied?" he wanted to know, arching his brows as he looked at her intently.

She was about to say something flippant but found herself drawn once more by the magnetism in his eyes and the beguiling smile on his lips.

"Salt," she said, holding up the shaker before him.

Mike began to laugh as he took it from her and proceeded to shake it over the warm kernels. "You're one of a kind, too," he told her.

Am I, she thought. She didn't answer.

"Mind if I take this off?" he asked, indicating his jacket.

"Why would I mind?" she asked guardedly.

"Why indeed?" he replied, his velvet eyes sweeping her slowly as if memorizing every inch of her body from her face down to her bare toes, which peeked out from her high-heeled sandals.

For a moment they sat and ate popcorn, listening to the rain. "What gave you the idea I was a womanizer?" Mike said suddenly.

"Oh, rumors," Kate replied vaguely.

"Any in particular?" he inquired casually.

"Well..." She hesitated. She didn't like repeating gossip. There had been one particularly juicy item involving the New York vice-president's wife. "I hear you don't care if a woman is married. Or even the wife of— the company brass," she finished lamely.

"Come again?"

"Well, the New York vice-president's wife," she said, reluctantly.

"What do they say about me and the v.p.'s wife?" He sounded mildly interested.

"Oh, that you and she carried on behind her husband's back while he worked closely with you. That sort of thing," she said offhandedly.

Mike began to laugh. Kate felt annoyed that he could look back at a past affair so flippantly. Was he a harder man than he appeared?

"Have you ever met Henry Idlewild?" he inquired, mentioning the vice-president's name. Kate knew it only from correspondence.

"No," she admitted.

"And I take it you've not met Mrs. Idlewild, either?"

She shook her head. Somehow he had managed to get his arm around her again. Talk about an operator, Kate thought.

"Mrs. Idlewild is closer to sixty than she would care to admit, and she weighs about two hundred pounds. I like them slimmer," he told Kate, keeping a straight face. "At least below one seventy."

"Really?" Kate grinned, not totally convinced that what he was saying was true. But his saying it made her feel happy all the same. She felt she had known him a long time. Certainly rapport had sprung up between them faster than with anyone she had ever known before. Even Ryan had proceeded more slowly, and he had had a very fixed goal. Goal. Kate narrowed her eyes a little as she pressed more popcorn on Mike. He shook his head, declining.

"Gets stuck in my teeth," he told her. "But you go ahead. You've got a ways to go to a hundred and seventy."

"Tell me, is this standard procedure with you, getting so intimate with your personnel?"

"I find it hard to think of you as personnel," he said, his words caressing her. "And if you think this is intimate, you're missing the boat. 'Intimate' has a very different meaning."

"And you're just the man to explain it to me," she countered, opening her eyes wide.

Mike raised his hand, as if making a pledge. "Guilty."

"I think you and the 'office agitator' will get off on a better footing if we proceed with caution."

"You don't strike me as the cautious type."

"You'd be surprised."

"Disappointed," he admitted. "Besides, cautious types don't send long petitions to the president of the company, demanding more money."

She shrugged, caught.

"Why did you do it?" Mike wanted to know. "You don't *look* like you're in financial need." He eyed the tastefully furnished room.

True, her action had provoked a minor cataclysm at Icon. She had been set upon by several representatives from the New York office as well as by the unhappy Baines. They had all asked her the same question. But when they had asked, she had felt on the defensive and under direct attack. When Mike asked her now, she felt as if he was genuinely curious to learn why someone in her position, one of authority and some prestige, would risk the wrath of the New York office by siding with file clerks and claims adjusters.

"It's the principle of the thing," she explained. "Besides, what would you do if twenty people came to you and said they were having trouble making ends meet, that they couldn't wait until the scheduled annual salary review came with its miniscule yearly raise? The salary scale at Icon is far behind the times."

To her surprise, Mike nodded. Was he just humoring her?

"I'd probably do the same thing," he told her, and she wasn't sure whether to believe him or not. But he sounded sincere. If he was, he was going to be a godsend for the office.

"What do you suggest we do if it doesn't stop raining?" he asked suddenly, switching the conversation back to them.

She knew exactly what he was thinking. No, she wasn't going to make it that easy for him, despite the fact that she wanted to be with him. If she gave in just like that, he might think it was a habit.

"I do have extra bedrooms," she offered reluctantly.

"They must be lonely," he said.

"Not once you're inside them," she said with a smile.

He seemed to like this game between them because he fell into the spirit of the thing. "Well, lucky for you it seems to be clearing up again." He glanced out the picture window. The large raindrops on the pane slid slowly down, unaided by any new rain. He rose and gave her a hand up. "How about dinner tomorrow?" he asked. "Saturday."

"Fine." She nodded, pleased.

"Great, what are you making?"

"I thought you were taking me out," she said, caught off guard.

"I'd rather be taking you in," he said, his voice soft and seductive. "Besides," he added, "I'm starved for a good home-cooked meal."

"Then you'll have to stay starved."

"You don't cook?" he asked, cocking his head.

"TV dinners and five-minute eggs," she said with a grin and a shrug. "And popcorn."

"Didn't your mother ever tell you the way to a man's heart is through his stomach?" Mike asked playfully, putting his arms about her slim shoulders.

"I don't think that was what you had in mind tonight," she said mischievously.

"No, my stomach was the farthest thing from my mind." He looked down into her face. His expression was warm. "Okay, you win—dinner out. Any special place?"

"I'll have one picked out by the time you get here," she promised, walking him to the inner door leading to the garage.

"Is seven too early?"

No, not early enough, she thought, a bright happiness glowing inside her. He kissed her once more, pressing her tightly against his tall frame. She could feel that the intensity of the moment was not one-sided as the bold outline of his body made her once more aware of the air of sexuality about him. The kiss was brief though intense, and soon Michael Fleming was getting into his open car and lifting a hand to her as he maneuvered out of the garage. Kate went back inside, feeling not entirely displeased with the way she'd handled things. Always leave them wanting more, her father had told her. Sean Logan had been referring to performing before an audience, but his words fit this occasion nonetheless. Mike Fleming had certainly left her wanting more.

She closed the door softly behind her, trying to force thoughts of him from her mind. For the umpteenth time she reminded herself that Mike was her boss, and that his instant attraction to her—to the neglect even of the office siren, Gay—might very well be a ruse to trap her into conduct unbecoming to a second assistant benefits manager.

But what was the reason for her own instant attraction, her mind questioned. Kate switched on the radio and tried to make her mind a peaceful blank.

As dusk fell Saturday, Kate slipped into a two-piece lavender suit that flattered her coloring and her slim figure and went over the events of the previous night in her mind. Was she on the verge of falling in love with her boss? It would be very foolish—especially since she was so unsure of his motives. Yet for years she'd been sure she hadn't survived the emotional scars of her marriage—that she would never again feel about a man the way she was feeling now. She supposed the situation had its positive aspects.

What a difference a little time could make, she mused, pulling a comb through her silvery blond hair and arranging it to fall softly about her shoulders. A month ago Baines had branded her a maverick, and she'd become the favorite victim of his tight-lipped assistant, a pasty-faced, pudgy man whose only daily exercise was to pick up jelly doughnuts and push intercom buttons. Now she had a date with the exciting new office manager himself, a confident, powerful man who promised to breathe life into a failing office while bringing the fresh air of excitement into her life.

Which could certainly use it, she thought dryly. The situation was growing stale about her, thick with management power struggles and bungled handling of the company accounts. But that didn't have to concern her as much as she'd been letting it. She was in Carson City for a limited time, for as long as it took to prove herself. She knew this wouldn't be her way of life forever. Once everything was settled in her mind, once she had accomplished the goals she had set for herself, she expected to return to California and the world she had left behind.

Why else had she joined the little theater group? Signing up with the amateur production company had stirred the beginnings of something within her. With little or no previous experience, and with no one knowing anything of her family ties, Kate had landed the leading role in *Rain*, the play based on Somerset Maugham's short story. It wasn't that she was sure she wanted to join the family profession—it was just that whatever she did, she wanted to be sure she'd proved she had the mettle to make it entirely on her own first. Coming to Carson City and rising from within the ranks at Icon Assurance had done just that. Perhaps it wouldn't be much longer...

But while she was at Icon, she told herself, giving her hair a final pat, she intended to do the very best job she could and to keep all her principles intact. She would oversee her unit as effectively as possible and look out for the people beneath her. None of this included being seduced by the boss—for whatever reason *he* might have.

Kate heard the doorbell ring downstairs, and her pulse quickened. He was here! She checked over her makeup and straightened her skirt, then turned quickly to make sure she had managed to catch all the buttons that ran down the back of her outfit. Ready.

"Your chariot, madam," Mike said, pointing toward his Mercedes, which still had its top down. Her hair, so carefully groomed moments earlier, whipped helter-skelter about her head as they drove to downtown Carson City. Kate had selected a pleasant restaurant that she had been to once or twice before.

"I look like a mess," she muttered as they came to a stop in the parking lot and she studied her reflection in her compact mirror.

"You look like a windblown gift from heaven," Mike amended, standing by the side of the car and waiting to help her out as she tried to comb the tangles into some sort of order.

"You're wasting your time as an office manager," she said. "With that suave tongue of yours, you could go far."

"Only your office manager temporarily," he emphasized. His words reminded her to keep a proper perspective on him. He wouldn't be here forever. He wouldn't be a permanent fixture in her life; more like a passing ship. And she was determined not to stay in dry dock because of him.

Mike ushered her inside to a table. He ordered for both of them and included a bottle of champagne. After they had finished their dinner, he ordered brandy. By then Kate's head was spinning. Mike had seemed far less interested in food or drink than he had in her. He had asked her question upon question—about the office, about herself, about scores of things. If she hadn't known better, she would have sworn she was under investigation. Many of these questions were extremely pointed, and while she answered them, she couldn't help wondering if she wasn't being too free, if the good food and alcohol hadn't loosened her tongue. She tried to read the expression in his eyes but couldn't. It seemed to waver from probing and business-like to a more familiar near-caress.

Kate sighed. Whatever his motivation for pressing her, the barrage of questions had helped make the time go by. Suddenly, glancing at her watch, she realized they had been talking for nearly three hours.

"Would you like anything else?" Mike asked, glancing at her empty dessert plate and at the brandy glass that had been refilled several times by an obliging waiter.

That Kate was tempted to say "You" confirmed that she'd had too much brandy. She felt giddy despite the ample meal, and although part of her lightheadedness was due to the potency of the alcohol, she knew the rest stemmed directly from the company she was keeping. She shook her head. "I'm fine," she murmured.

"Okay, time to get you back," he said, as if his life was already on a timetable. Via the grapevine Kate had heard that while he was at work, Mike liked to run a very tight schedule. But this was Saturday night. They weren't on a schedule now. Or were they? Was this all part of some vast plan of his to get things under control? People used the tools best available to them, and certainly Mike had plenty of charm.

As they drove back to her place, she caught herself wishing that the car didn't have bucket seats. She would have loved to curl up next to him, to pretend that he wasn't who he was and she wasn't who she was but that they were just two people getting to know each other. She sighed.

"Anything wrong?" he asked, glancing her way.

All about them the bright budding green of April was passing them swiftly.

"Not a thing," she replied.

Mike's smile deepened.

She felt the smile having a heady effect on her, making her warm and producing an intimate glow. The champagne, she thought again. She shouldn't have had so much.

Mike pulled the Mercedes into her driveway and helped her out. "When did you say your chaperon was due back?" he asked, taking her key from her hand and opening the door.

"Gladys? Oh, she usually comes back sometime after midnight." She checked her watch. It was just past eleven. "It's part of this package bus deal," she explained in an attempt to hide the nervous thrill that was beginning to take hold of her. "She goes off with a group of women she knows and they gamble all night and straight into the next day, filling themselves up on the complimentary food while they're at it. Gladys comes back dead tired, usually a lot poorer, and weighing five pounds more than when she left." Kate laughed.

"Doesn't sound very pleasant," Mike said, closing the door behind him.

"She loves it," Kate told him with a shrug. His eyes held hers, and she felt a wave of electricity pass between them. It was as though she had touched a live wire.

"You're tense," he said, taking her by the hand and leading her to the sofa in the den.

"I'm slightly tipsy," she corrected.

The grin on his face broadened. "That sounds promising."

"Promises," Kate echoed, sinking down next to him on the oversize cushions. "I bet you're the type who doesn't make promises," she said knowingly.

"None that I can't keep," he confirmed.

At least he was honest. Hadn't she said she liked honesty? But where was she headed? Part of her was falling headlong for this fantastically attractive man. Caution, she told herself. Caution.

"I like your suit," Mike murmured. Bending over, he kissed the side of her neck. "But isn't it hard to get in and out of?" he asked, his hand lightly flicking against the row of buttons marching up her back.

"I manage."

"I hate to see a lady struggle," he told her gallantly,

his hand still resting against the buttons, now gently playing with the top one.

"I wasn't aware that I was taking it off," she said, sharply.

"*You're* not," he told her, nibbling her ear. His breath tantalized her, bringing out a strong response from her that surprised her with its intensity.

Mike's hand slipped behind her shoulder blades and attempted expertly to relieve her from the confines of the brief jacket while he kissed her face ever so lightly. A churning sensation was beginning within her as her fingertips turned icy cold. But she struggled to stop him.

"I think your inspection of office personnel should stop here," she cautioned with effort. "There's nothing to be gained by this."

"Oh, I don't know . . ." Mike said softly, kissing her shoulder through the fabric. It felt as if there were no barrier at all.

"And I'm not to be scaled so easily . . ." Kate was continuing, trying desperately to put her mind elsewhere. Anything but to give in to the demands of her body.

Mike raised his head momentarily, a smile flickering across his lips. "I became a troubleshooter because it wasn't easy to get inside a problem and remedy it. I love a challenge."

A challenge? Was she just an exercise to display his prowess? A computer game to conquer? His words gave her the fuel she needed to withdraw from the fiery worlds into which she was swiftly descending.

"Do you like to lose?" she asked tersely.

"I don't know," he told her honestly, his eyes still raking her body.

"Why?" she asked with a forced laugh, moving away from him. "Haven't you formed an opinion?"

"No," he answered, the smile returning. "I've never lost," he said simply.

She squared her shoulders defensively. Her subconscious knew she was in serious trouble. "Is that a warning?"

"That, dear lady," he said, running a tantalizing finger along her lips, "is a promise."

Searching desperately for something to put him off with, she moved even farther back on the sofa and cocked her head. "You said you're to be temporary—is that why you're working so fast?"

"We each march to the drummer we hear," he told her, his eyes dancing as he brushed away the silvery wave of hair that had fallen into her eyes.

"Well, the music has just stopped," she said firmly, sounding stronger than she felt. Her insides quivered nervously. If only his eyes weren't so velvetlike, his smile so enticingly wicked, and his touch so like heaven... A struggle raged within her, but she forged on.

"Why are you only temporary?" she continued, pressing him. "It doesn't make sense. Usually when they get rid of one office manager, they replace him with another—until he messes up," she added.

It was true, though. That Mike should be a temporary replacement didn't make sense to her. It had bothered her from the moment she had heard the announcement.

To Kate's surprise, she saw the expression on Mike's face change subtly. It was more closed than it had been a moment ago, as if he had just remembered something. Then his gaze sharpened, reminding her of the grilling in the restaurant. Suddenly there was a barrier between them. He shrugged.

"I guess New York thinks I'm too valuable to live in any one place for an extended period of time. My job," he told her, rising, "is to step into a troubled area and right the wrong. Kind of like Captain Midnight," he

added with a grin. Apparently he had decided to make
light of the situation.

Or Superman, Kate thought. She couldn't take her
eyes off his body as he shrugged back into his jacket.
He was no stranger to the rigors of exercise, she judged.
No one looked that terrific by the graces of nature alone.

"Lucky for you I have an appointment first thing tomorrow," he said.

"An appointment?" she echoed. "On Sunday?"

"A good Icon employee does not allow himself to be
swayed by the calendar. Your soul," he said, his eyes
twinkling, "belongs to the demands of the job."

"I thought only doctors were supposed to feel that
way," Kate said, rising.

"I *am* a doctor," he told her. "I'm supposed to take
a sick office and put it back on its feet."

"I can tell you what's wrong with it," Kate volunteered, "other than the obvious, the loss of our big accounts."

Mike nodded as he slipped his shoes on. "All in good
time. I'm coming in on Monday," he told her. "We'll
hold a general meeting with Baines and the rest of you
management types," he said, touching the tip of her nose,
"and try to hash it all out."

Moments later Mike was back in the Mercedes, giving
Kate a casual toss of his hand as he maneuvered the car
out of the driveway. Strange, she thought, watching him
through the picture window. You'd've thought he'd want
to talk about it ahead of time. By the time she'd turned
that one over in her mind, he was gone.

It was several hours before Gladys returned. Kate had
gone to bed but found herself lying awake, unable to
sleep. But she waited till the next morning to confront
the housekeeper. The short, henna-haired woman was
excited about her winning streak. But Kate hardly heard
a thing she said. Her mind was still on Mike. Her unsettled state even interfered with her concentration when

she studied her lines that afternoon for the little theater play. She still couldn't believe she had snatched the lead in *Rain*, playing the free-spirited prostitute Sadie Thompson. Normally she could emote with a verve that was missing in her day-to-day life. But her mind refused to concentrate. The puzzle Mike represented kept coming back. Why was he temporary? And was he truly interested in her, or was there another motive to his sensual attacks?

# CHAPTER
## *Three*

MONDAY MORNING KATE came in early, as was her habit. As management, she had her own key to the office and was usually there before anyone. It was part of her orderly nature. She liked getting an early start, relishing the peacefulness of the morning. And a small part of her was hoping that Mike would come in early as well.

Kate began to organize her day's work slowly, aided by a strong cup of coffee. She found herself glancing up every time she perceived a shadow of a figure crossing the office. She was waiting for him all right, she thought, annoyed with herself. She had all but logically convinced herself that there was some ulterior motive to his attentiveness, and for that reason she felt she had to view him in a guarded manner. Now if she could only convince her racing pulse of that...

Gay arrived at almost nine, just before the last shift was due. The hours were staggered so the office was staffed from seven in the morning to five in the evening.

Yet Gay often arrived at nine and left as early as three. No one found fault with her. She was friendly with Asherton, and Kate had decided that must carry a lot of weight.

The lovely Eurasian woman wore a sleek white suit that contrasted sharply with her dark polished hair. Though the suit jacket was well cut and businesslike, Kate noted that it did little to hide Gay's ample cleavage. Kate smiled to herself. Obviously Gay was anticipating Mike's arrival as well.

Gay approached Kate, smiling buoyantly. Kate braced herself anyway. Gay had looked definitely upset with her for leaving the party on Friday with Mike.

"Get home all right?" Gay asked, slipping gracefully into a seat next to Kate's neatly stacked desk.

Kate opened her mouth to answer, but Gay was obviously not interested in getting a response to her question. "He's a nice-looking man, isn't he?" she said significantly.

Kate wasn't surprised by Gay's confidential tone. Although the women could not be called close, in the office, perhaps because of their shared rank, Gay often used Kate as a semiconfidante and sought her out each time she became involved with a new man—which happened with regular frequency, Kate had observed. Now the roles were reversed.

"You mean Mike Fleming?" Kate asked, trying for a casual tone.

Gay's smile remained intact. "Yes, I do mean Mike. Who else in this office could possibly fit that description?" True, of the handful of males that populated the office, none deserved a second glance, much less a warm response.

"You sound like you're falling for him," Kate said, trying to keep a disinterested lilt to her voice.

Gay's dark eyes danced. "Oh, I wouldn't go *that* far..." her voice trailed off suggestively. "Frankly, I thought you had him sewn up when he took you home Friday."

"Now Gay, I—" Kate began to protest.

But Gay wouldn't be interrupted. "Of course, when he dropped by my place yesterday..."

The words stabbed through the Monday morning air, hitting Kate like a physical blow. "He—dropped by?" she asked with a dry throat.

"Well, he *had* arranged it in advance. It was quite early, you see." Gay raised her brows significantly. "We had a lovely breakfast. I enjoyed it immensely, even if he did ask me more questions than any other man I've met. He seems to want to know *everything* about me. Though it's not an entirely unattractive quality..." Her voice was melodious, gaining in rhythm and soft intensity. Kate knew that tone. Gay was ready to launch into a detailed personal account. Kate waved her to a halt.

"Gay, do you mind?" she asked, her voice sounding hollow to her own ears. "I've got a lot of work to do." She gestured at the piles of medical claims that surrounded her desk-top computer. Monday was the heaviest day of the week, starting out with mail that had been accumulating for three days at the local post office box.

Gay rose, visibly annoyed at having been cut off. "He's a smooth operator," she said significantly.

Kate nodded, her eyes still on the papers before her. He sure was. The rat. For reasons she didn't quite allow herself to fathom, she would have vastly preferred that Mike be a straightforward, uncomplicated man, simply pushy and lustful. But seeing two of his female subordinates at the same time? The trace of mystery and intrigue she had sensed about him from the first returned tenfold. So what if he had sent her pulse racing for a brief moment? He was a man to be dealt with carefully. He was a man who was not what he seemed. Kate sighed as Gay clicked away on her stylish heels, just a trifle higher than office decorum would suggest. She told herself it was best that she did feel leery of Michael Fleming. He was her boss, even if temporarily, and she had no business becoming romantically entwined with him.

Well, why had he gone on to Gay? Couldn't he have at least let a day go by before he continued his comparison shopping for a lover? Kate knew she was jumping to conclusions. But she had seen that smile on Gay's face before and had heard about her trysts. Despite her resolve to stay cool, Kate couldn't bear to hear the woman describe making love to Mike in glowing terms.

Light, keep it light, Kate warned herself. She had been right about him after all. But somehow being right brought no particular pleasure.

Kate found it terribly hard to concentrate for the remainder of the morning, even though the green light from her computer demanded her attention and the telephone hardly ever ceased its urgent peal. It was Monday, and the entire world had been set loose with its various problems. Everyone had her number.

Lunch was her only solitude. Kate went to the parking lot and climbed into the Porsche. From a large leather bag she extracted a copy of *Rain* and without further ado began to absorb herself in the play. With an eye to her own lines, she forced herself into a different time, a different place, a different world—the world of Sadie Thompson. It was not an easy world, yet it eased the turmoil in her mind.

When Kate closed the script forty-five minutes later, she had committed her lines in the first act to memory by sheer will. She got out of the car. It was time to go back.

"Going my way?"

A wave of uncontrollable excitement passed over her as she felt his presence. Be calm, Kate. Easier said than done, was her next thought. But her acting stood her in good stead.

"I'm going back to the office, if that's what you mean," she said coldly.

"That's what I mean," he said, holding the glass door open for her. "Doing work on your lunch hour?" His eyes indicated the bulky script under her arm.

She hugged the item closer to her, not wanting him to see what it was. She hadn't even realized that she had brought it with her. Normally she left it in the car. "No, this is pleasure," she said, making no attempt to show it to him.

They stepped into the elevator, and he reached across her to press number eight. Very aware of his closeness, she took a step to the side, wondering why he was crowding her when there was so much space to be had. Three women entered on the third floor, casting appreciative glances in Mike's direction.

"Why so distant?" he asked as they got off together, the words feathering across her cheek.

"I have a lot on my mind," she said succinctly. "It's Monday, our heavy day," she added, fearing she had seemed overly rude.

But he looked unruffled, nodding as if suddenly remembering the fact. "That's right. I'll get into the routine of this soon enough."

"I think you already have," she couldn't resist muttering. She knew he had heard her.

He didn't react, though. He held the navy blue door with its light blue lettering proclaiming Icon Assurance open for her. She felt his eyes on her as she walked in front of him, and despite herself, a warm wave went over her. She caught herself allowing her hips to sway a little. Maybe Sadie Thompson was getting to her, she thought with a smile creeping to her lips. She was as bad as Gay. Besides, hadn't she tried to forestall anything intimate? What *was* she thinking of? She had just branded him as a philanderer. What did she want with someone who spelled trouble no matter which way she looked at it?

Everything, her soul whispered before she could turn a deaf ear to her feelings. Everything.

She stopped for a moment, and Mike didn't. Consequently he bumped into her, knocking the script from her hand. Before she could make a move, he had bent to pick it up, his green eyes scanning the cover. *Rain,* it announced in bold letters. His expression puzzled, he handed the script back to her.

"Extracurricular reading," she mumbled, searching her mind for a better excuse but finding none. It was, after all, her first play. She wanted no one to learn of it. When she'd mastered it, proved herself, why, then she'd let others know. Till then it was her own little secret. That way if she failed, no one would be the wiser.

With that Kate turned her back on Mike and marched down the long row of files that led to her desk. She noted that eyes were passing her by and focusing on the man she had left behind. As she dropped script and purse into her bottom drawer, she too turned to watch Mike enter Baines's office.

Kate tried to shut out the noise and speculation about Mike that seemed to be rising on all sides of her. Normally her group was rather a quiet one, but today wasn't a normal day. It wasn't every day that someone like Mike Fleming appeared. Kate smiled to herself as she turned her attention to the top file on her desk and switched on her computer. Sorting out the work and finding the necessary codes, she proceeded to type in the information on the keyboard, watching the green letters spring up on the screen. A second assistant manager wasn't actually expected to work medical claims, but Kate had found that because of the speed with which she managed to finish her regular duties, she had a great deal of time left over. So, unlike Gay, Kate pitched in to ease the work load within her group whenever she found a chance. And today it looked as if she was the only one working. Things had virtually ground to a halt around her.

Finally Kate saw the reason why.

Baines was bringing Mike around to all the desks, which in itself was rather unusual. Normally someone in Mike's position was introduced only to management. Clearly Mike was being introduced to everyone.

Kate stopped what she was doing and watched. She heard Baines trip over names, and he looked quite befuddled at times. His memory had never been good. It was getting harder and harder to hide her amusement. Mike repeated each name slowly, as if he was memorizing it along with the face before him. Few of the women remained cool around him, and almost everyone responded to his show of warmth.

When it came to be her turn, Mike gave her a deep, warm smile as the balding, awkward Baines mumbled, "And of course, this is Miss Lonigan."

"Of course," Mike murmured, as if sharing a private joke with Kate.

Kate's resolve to be strictly professional dissolved as she met his eyes. He could conquer nations with those eyes, she cautioned herself, looking away.

When she looked up again, Mike was already making his way to the next unit—Gay's unit. She saw him stop to talk to Gay. Then he retreated with Gay and Baines to his office. The last thing Kate saw was the door closing behind them. Now what?

But she didn't have time to ponder. The phone rang once again. Soon another insured client was spilling out his story to her. So involved was she with the pleading voice on the other end of the line as she keyed in code numbers to call up his records that Kate didn't realize that Mike was standing over her until she'd hung up. She had assumed that whoever was at her elbow was one of the claims adjusters. They were used to waiting until she completed a call before giving them her attention.

Kate looked up in surprise.

"Now that you're finished," Mike said with a patient smile, "I'd like to see you in Al's office for a few minutes."

She rose as bidden, snapping off her computer. "Why didn't you interrupt me?" she asked. "I would have called the person back."

"Best to handle each call as it comes in. That way clients don't feel as if you're putting them off. You sounded very professional—as well as kind," he added just before he opened the door to the office for her.

"I am professional," she told him.

"And kind?"

"To stray animals and helpless people," she said, trying to force down a smile.

"I'll keep that in mind," he told her, ushering her inside. The feel of his hand on her back did terrible things to her. She tried to hide the effect he was having but then made the mistake of glancing up into his eyes. For a moment she was lost—but not before determining that what was happening was not one-sided. Mike's smile had the intimacy of a caress; his eyes probed hers. For another instant she allowed herself to be transported as the world seemed to fade around her. Then she remembered that Mike Fleming was not exclusive in dispensing his favors. Gay Ling could easily have produced the same effect in him. That thought brought Kate smartly back to attention. Her eyes straight ahead, she preceded Mike into the office.

There the other managers sat waiting for them. Dave Martin, the first assistant manager, displayed a sullen expression he wasn't quick enough to mask. He was a man in his early thirties, with little imagination but high ambition at Icon. Kate knew he had expected to get Baines's position. Milt Peters, Kate's other peer as second assistant manager, sat next to Gay. She was the most animated of the group; her eyes riveted on Mike as he lowered himself into Baines's chair. The outgoing office manager meekly took a seat next to Kate.

Mike regarded each of them slowly before he began. "The first thing I want to impress upon you is that you're all part of one whole. This office is a unit—one unit, not three," he emphasized carefully. "We're all going to work together to make sure this is a smooth-working machine. That doesn't mean to say that I view anyone as a cog," he said pointedly, looking at each of the three unit leaders. "Each piece has a function. If that function breaks down, I want to know the whys and wherefores. I think personally, from the little I've observed, that the difficulty here is that a lot of the problems have been swept under the rug and not examined for causes. That makes for a very lumpy rug and no progress to speak of. I'm here to make progress."

"Good," Gay said with a suggestive smile.

Mike overlooked the comment, but Kate did not. Gay was already beginning to flaunt their relationship. And it was only a few hours old! An unbidden spark of anger made her head throb.

"All right, I want to hear from each of you as to what you think the problems are here," Mike said, leaning back in his chair.

The others were only too happy to tell him. The discussion ran on for some time. Essentially Gay and Dave, the first assistant manager, told Mike that they got no respect or support from the employees.

"They're mostly lazy," complained Dave. "They want to coast by on as little work as possible. A call for overtime brings no volunteers. They take too many sick days. They're late, sloppy, and foul up more claims than they process. By the time a halfway decent employee has gotten enough experience to be of any use, he or she moves on to another company."

Mike said nothing, listening to all the points quietly. Finally he turned to Kate, who sat watching Mike's reaction to the others' words with intent curiosity.

"You haven't said anything," he told her. "What do you think is wrong with the office?"

"Morale is down," Kate said, beginning slowly. Watching the others out of the corner of her eye, she saw Dave smirk. "The employees are underpaid, overworked, not praised for their accomplishments, and not listened to if they have complaints."

"There she goes again," Dave said, gesturing impatiently.

Mike gave Dave a glance, and he quickly closed his mouth.

"Go on," Mike prompted somberly.

"You've got to give the employees a sense of satisfaction. There has to be some kind of a—a reward, if you will, for hard work, other than more hard work," Kate insisted, warming to her subject.

"She's always taking their side," Dave said dismissively.

Kate turned on him, finally voicing her feelings. "Well, someone has to." With effort she lowered her voice. "You create a happy crew and you'll have an office that puts out. Then maybe you'll see those numerical quotas everyone's so eager for."

"They're issued by the home office," Dave protested.

"Fine. But if the adjusters felt they were getting something for meeting such high quotas . . ." Kate pointed out, letting her voice trail away. She thought about how unrealistic the situation was. The home office in New York expected the claims processors to work 88 percent of the incoming claims within five days of receipt, no matter how much mail came in.

"They get their paychecks," Gay said.

"They can get those anywhere," Kate countered. "Why stay here? We don't create an atmosphere that makes them want to stay."

"Like piped in music and a sauna?" Dave suggested sarcastically.

"Like understanding," Kate persisted.

Dave turned to Mike. "We're not here to coddle them. They do their job, no excuses, or out they go," he said proudly.

Kate only shook her head, giving up on arguing with Dave. He was hopeless. She looked toward Mike, wondering if he would disappoint her and agree with Dave.

But Mike nodded thoughtfully. "I'll take what each of you has said into consideration. Al, would you mind if I used your office for a few minutes?" he asked, turning the chair so he could look at the meek man off to the side.

Baines shook his red-fringed head. "No, no, use it as long as you like. It'll be yours soon anyway."

Mike smiled his thanks. "That's all for now," he said, dismissing the group. "Kate, would you mind staying behind?" he asked as she reached for the doorknob.

Gay looked at Kate carefully but exited after only a moment's pause, flanked by Milt and Dave. The stunning, dark-haired woman smiled confidently. Perhaps she thought Kate was about to be reprimanded for her outspoken views. Kate wondered if Gay was right.

"Good to have you with us," Dave said, turning to shake Mike's hand at the door. "I believe we'll get this office back on course."

"Oh, we'll do that all right," Mike said confidently. Dave appeared satisfied as he left the room.

"Shut the door," Mike instructed Kate. She closed it behind her and stood regarding him for a moment.

"Relax," he said with a smile. "This isn't a Roman arena."

She thought about the departing people. "You could have fooled me," she murmured. He said nothing for a moment, as if regarding the notes he had taken while the others vented their views. She looked at the way the sun caressed his tanned features and wondered where he could have gotten such a deep tan in New York, it being the middle of the summer notwithstanding.

Once again her eyes went slowly over his chiseled features, the high cheekbones and slightly gaunt face, the sensuous mouth. His black lashes intrigued her as he focused his eyes on the notes. What would it be like, a small voice echoed within her, to see herself reflected in those eyes, to have those eyes behold her with something other than mischief in them? A hot flush coursed through her veins as her mind ordered her to remember that this man was her company superior and should be viewed as such before all else—as if that made it any easier.

Mike looked up, seeming to sense her eyes on him. He gave her an easy smile. "You look like you're about to spring into battle," he commented, his eyes sweeping over her.

She relaxed a little. "I'm used to being attacked in this office," she replied with a small smile.

Mike chuckled. "That might not be a bad idea, but not during office hours. Besides," he continued, "I never attack. Mutual pleasure is much more my style."

She nodded a bit self-consciously. Was he teasing her? Could he sense what she was thinking?

"I take it you don't agree with the others on how the office should be run. Since you're outnumbered, why do you stay?" he asked bluntly.

She squared her shoulders slightly. "Challenge, I suppose. I don't give up easily."

His smile spread. "Neither do I."

"Well," she said when he made no effort to say anything further, "am I here to be chastised?"

"For what?" he asked, folding his arms and waiting for an explanation.

"Chastised," she repeated. "You know, being told to hold my tongue. Put in my place." Her smile faded just a touch. "As the company rabble rouser, as Mr. Baines called me. The troublemaker," she prompted when he didn't respond. "I warn you, though, I've been lectured to by the best. New York sent someone out not more than a month ago for the express purpose of defusing me. Placating me was the tactic he chose—kind words and not one single concession. I think," she added, "he was afraid I was going to start a union because of that cost-of-living petition. Perhaps I should."

"Whoa," Mike said lightly. "I don't believe in placation. Or speeches."

She wished he would look elsewhere rather than straight at her. Baines had always looked at his hands and Asherton past her head. Mike's steady gaze almost made her want to flinch—not from its directness but because again she was drowning in the steely green of his eyes, wanting to say things to him that had nothing at all to do with work or the subject at hand.

"Besides," Mike continued softly, "I agree with you and I could use your help to straighten out the impossible mess your office is in." She was surprised and uncertain of whether to take his words at face value. Obviously he saw the doubt in her eyes. "My, but you're the skeptic."

"I told you, I've been lied to by the best."

Mike came around to the front of his desk and looked down at her. One large hand brushed gently against her face. He regarded her thoughtfully. "I've no doubt," he said, and she knew that he wasn't talking about work.

For one moment they stood, he making no effort to back away and she held fast by the power of his presence. Kate thought her knees would give way and willed herself to look impersonal, while her heart beat hard and somewhere within her her emotions pleaded that he hold her fast again.

"And"—his breath ruffled the hair on her forehead as it fell in a wave across her right eye; he brushed it away with his fingertips, almost caressing the skin he touched beneath—"you seem to be the only one in this office who thinks the way I do."

"If that's a line—" she began boldly.

"The only lines are in that script of yours," he assured her. "I'm serious." His voice became more businesslike again. "Your office is in big trouble. Many large accounts are threatening to leave. The home office is seriously thinking of closing you down and sending the remaining accounts elsewhere. Production is down, consumer complaints are up, and we're losing money as well as face. Now whatever they've been doing here has obviously not worked," he continued, "but it isn't all that unique in business." He backed away slightly and leaned against his desk. "Most American businesses make the mistake of treating their people as expendable, then wonder why there's such a large turnover."

Kate watched him, intrigued. She was beginning to believe he meant what he said. If nothing else, he certainly sounded sincere. But the situation didn't look bright for Icon, Carson City. "So you're saying that there's no solution to the problem, just business as usual?" she ventured.

"No, quite the opposite. I'm saying we should begin to change the structure of the situation." He smiled. "Just as you suggested."

"I've been shouting into the wind," she reminded him gently.

The smile grew broader. "But your voice has carried."

They looked at one another for a moment and then smiled.

"So what do you propose to do?" she asked.

"I'm not official here until Thursday," he told her. "For tonight I propose to take you out to dinner."

Despite all the well-worded arguments that came to mind, Kate was sorely tempted. But fate was out to keep her in check, even if she wasn't. Darn, she thought. There was a rehearsal tonight. "I'm afraid I'm busy tonight," she told him.

Mike shrugged, too easily for her satisfaction. "Some other time, then."

She nodded. "Some other time," she echoed, leaving his office and returning to her desk. But she couldn't get back to work. His presence teased her mind during the rest of the day. Vivid recollections of their last kiss kept cropping up, coupled with the unsettling impression made by his magnetic eyes. It was as if he had enlisted something within her to torture her.

You made a commitment to the play, she reminded herself sternly, and don't need to get yourself involved in an emotionally volatile situation.

At that moment Gay passed Kate's desk in her immaculate white suit. The lovely brunet paused, regarding Kate and then her own perfectly manicured nails. "He asked me out to dinner," she said softly.

"Congratulations," Kate said shortly.

"What were you and Mike discussing earlier?" Gay asked, sitting down without an invitation. Kate willed her to go away.

"We didn't talk," she said, directing her attention to the claim under her hand. "We made love on the desk and then I said I'd see him around."

She glanced back at Gay, who looked stunned. Then the woman laughed delicately. "You're very witty, Kate."

"That's me," Kate muttered. "The office wit." She looked up just in time to see Mike leaving the office. He waved in their direction. Gay gave him a languid smile. Kate acknowledged him with a curt nod.

What was going on here, she wondered.

"Shouldn't you be applying yourself to the monthly audit?" Kate asked as Gay stared after Mike. "By my calculations, you're at least a month behind."

"I'm not worried," Gay told her silkily. "How do you think I'll look in Dave Martin's office?" Kate felt her face flushing. The nerve of this woman! Flaunting her relationship with Mike, and now hinting that she would use it to get a promotion! Gay was really the pits. Kate lowered her head.

"About as good as Dave," she replied in more even tones than her state of mind warranted.

Gay didn't seem to notice the sarcasm. Presently, when Kate did not look up from her work, Gay departed silently. Kate held her pencil still for a moment, thinking. Then she continued to write.

# CHAPTER
# *Four*

REHEARSAL THAT NIGHT sapped all Kate's energy. She returned to her house thoroughly tired and slipped off her high heels as she stood at the front door. The soft, thick mocha pile of the carpet greeted her toes like a comforting old friend, and she sighed.

Gladys peeked out from around the kitchen area. "So, you're finally home."

"Looks that way, doesn't it?" Kate said. She walked slowly toward the first chair in the living room and sank into it like a rag doll. She wondered dully if she had enough oomph to make it to her bedroom or would just spend the night in the chair.

"I kept dinner for you," Gladys said.

"Save it. I'm too tired to chew. Besides," Kate added, rotating her neck slowly in an effort to get the kinks out of it, "I had a hamburger during rehearsal."

Kate felt Gladys's capable fingers begin to knead the ache away. Kate sighed in gratitude and relief.

"You know, I ought to be wringing your neck instead of massaging it," Gladys told her, her raspy voice stern.

"Now what have I done?" Kate asked. She was used to this from Gladys.

"Well, if you're really serious about acting, why won't you give your father a call and—"

"No," Kate said, putting her hands firmly on top of Gladys's plump ones, stopping her from any further movement. "I just want to dabble for the time being, without his help or his criticism. It took me two years to convince him that I could make it without his money— except for your salary," she added.

"Which is peanuts," Gladys interjected.

"A few more peanuts than *I* can afford at the moment, but it makes Dad happy to have you haunt me," Kate said fondly. She glanced up at Gladys's face. "Now you're not to call him either, okay?" Gladys did not answer. "Okay?" Kate repeated. This time her voice was a little firmer.

"Yeah, sure, it's your life," the woman said, shrugging. "If you want to spend it slaving in an insurance company, that's your business."

"I'm not slaving," Kate said, attempting to rise and then stopping. Her legs didn't seem to want to follow her.

"Hmph. I see you working on weekends, going in early, coming home late, and for what? To be called out on the carpet time and again by those feebleminded jerks? Ah, Katie, you've got talent," the woman said, sitting down on part of the cushion and taking Kate's hand in both of hers.

"A lot you know." Kate laughed. "According to the director, I'm three steps away from hopeless."

Gladys looked annoyed. "He's just some aspiring two-bit director. Why, your father—"

"Is to be kept out of it—as are my brothers," Kate warned, knowing the way Gladys's mind worked. "I want this solo flight to be just that—solo."

Rehearsing for her first play had both frightened Kate and electrified her senses. This was her family's world, and she was treading lightly. She wanted to succeed, to prove herself worthy before she let any of them know about her efforts. There was no way to keep it from Gladys, but she could certainly keep the housekeeper from spreading the news. She gave Gladys a significant glare.

Gladys muttered something under her breath that Kate couldn't catch and shuffled off to her own bedroom, her fluffy slippers dusting the fancy tiled floor as she went.

Kate sighed, shook her head, and followed suit. She was asleep before her head hit the pillow.

Wednesday's rehearsal was just as demanding. And then it was Thursday. Baines had left the office the day before, with little ceremony. The home office had given him another—slightly lower—position back East, where he had come from. He hadn't looked sorry to leave. The small, barren office that was the domain of the office manager now awaited his successor.

Kate found herself waiting, too.

Bright and early Thursday morning, before any of the other employees appeared, Mike walked in, a bright, color-blasted abstract painting under his arm and a heavy briefcase swinging from his hand. Kate looked up from her desk and rose to join him.

"Well, good morning," he said cheerfully. "Do you sleep here during the week?" He glanced up at the clock that hung on the far wall. It was twenty to seven.

"I come in early," she replied, catching the briefcase that slipped out of his hands as he tried to fish out his keys.

"Such diligence should be rewarded," he told her as he made his way to his new office.

"It's not locked," she told him. "He didn't leave anything worth taking," she added, following him in. She put the briefcase down on Mike's desk and turned to regard him as he held up the painting behind the desk.

"How does this look?" he asked.

"Cheerful."

He laughed. "Good. That's why I brought it. This place needs cheering up. You can be my goodwill ambassador," he said, taking off his jacket and opening his briefcase. He took out a hammer and two nails, then proceeded to hammer in the nails.

"The maintenance man could do that for you," Kate pointed out. "And you seem to be spreading goodwill without my help." She couldn't erase the touch of cynicism from her tone.

"Meaning?" he asked, not turning from his task.

"Gay Ling mentioned the wonderful time she had at dinner the other night," Kate said offhandedly.

"We talked business," he said casually.

"Gay always means business," Kate said cattily and then regretted it. Backstabbing never endeared you to anyone.

She watched the way Mike's muscles rippled beneath his shirt, feeling an unbidden response rise in her own body. She had planned to be cryptic with him. How dare he play her off against Gay? Yet when she was in his presence, her well-formed plans tended to fly from her mind.

Mike turned to study her. She was wearing a form-fitting shirtwaist dress, and his eyes showed their approval. "I asked you to join me first," he reminded her matter-of-factly.

"Yes, you did," she said briskly, trying to cover her unease, hoping she didn't look like a total fool. "Well, unless you need me for anything, I'll get back to my desk." She had begun to step out when his eyes stopped her.

"Can I hold you to that?" he asked in a low voice.

"To what?"

"That if I need you, you'll be there."

"I'm always there to do my job," she said quietly, then turned on her heels and left.

Mike followed her from his office, but it wasn't to continue their conversation. Rather, he seemed more interested in the files that were housed in the cabinet Baines had kept locked—the personnel files. Kate was surprised to see that Mike already had his own key to them. Baines had left acquiring such items up to his secretary. Obviously Mike left nothing to anyone but himself.

She watched him curiously from across the room as he went to the first drawer and took out some of the folders. Then he returned to his office and shut the door. For someone who was going to be here only temporarily, he did get into the job, Kate thought, then realized that if she didn't complete the transaction she had been working on when Mike came in, her computer would automatically log itself off and shut down, losing the numbers she had fed into it.

For the next few minutes she occupied herself with attempting to pay a substantial hospital bill. She didn't pick up the telephone that sounded shrilly until well past the second ring. Before she could give her customary greeting, she heard Mike's voice on the other end. She had been concentrating so hard she'd forgotten that she wasn't alone in the office, as she normally was in the morning. The fizzle on the line told her that this was a long-distance call. Their Watts line left a lot to be desired.

"How are you coming with your investigation?" said the terse voice on the other end of the line. Kate's hand froze as her eyes darted toward Mike's office. Investigation? An office manager wasn't supposed to do that.

"So far I've come up with nothing, but I'm working on several angles. I'll give you a call as soon as I know anything," she heard Mike promise.

Very carefully she replaced the phone in its cradle,

then stared thoughtfully in Mike's direction. From the start she had thought it odd that he was "temporary." The whole situation had not sat well with her. So. What could there possibly be here to investigate? The reason for the loss of accounts was simple enough: disorganization, incompetence, low morale. Kate stared at the green characters on her computer. Was something else going on here as well? And what "angles" was Mike working on? Was she just part of his investigation? Was he investigating how quickly a conquest of the women at Icon's Nevada office could be accomplished by an agent of the parent insurance company? The thought brought the merest of smiles. Then she looked back at the computer. Seriously, though, something was going on here, something more than met the eye. She wanted to know what it was about and how it would affect her.

Soon afterward the office began to come alive with personnel arriving in various numbers, all falling quiet as they reached their desks. Voices dropped to a whisper, sending a low hum about the room that mingled rather inharmoniously with the click of keys on desk computers. Mike came out shortly and walked slowly about the large L-shape room.

Kate could watch him from the vantage point she had at the center of the L. He stood off behind each group of workers and watched quietly. From what she could see, he wasn't saying anything.

This went on for over an hour. Each time she looked up from her work, there he was behind someone else, observing. What *was* he looking for? Finally he went back to his office.

Two minutes later her phone buzzed, indicating an inside call. "Kate Lonigan," she said into the receiver.

"I'd like to see you in my office," Mike's deep voice said.

Had he heard her pick up the phone before? Was she in for some more questions? She saw Dave Martin entering Mike's office, followed by the third unit leader, Milt Peters. Perhaps there was a simpler explanation. "Is this a meeting?" she asked.

"I like bright women," Mike's voice said an octave lower.

Then what were you doing with Gay, she wanted to ask but stopped herself just in time. "I'll be right there," she told him. "Flattery wins again."

Gay entered the office and took the seat closest to Mike, her dark eyes shimmering invitingly as she spread her crisp lavender dress about her trim legs. Kate regarded her angrily. Gay's merest gesture was suggestive, she felt. How come men never saw through her, anyway? How come Mike didn't?

For his part, Mike appeared to be aware of the lovely woman, but the look on his face showed Kate that he was more concerned with the business at hand, whatever that should prove to be.

Kate took a seat to the right, next to the window, and focused her eyes on Dave Martin. The first assistant appeared ready to stand at Mike's side for the duration of the meeting.

Mike glanced up from his chair. "Sit down, Dave," he said quietly.

So, Kate thought, Mike was aware of the second-in-command image that Dave was trying to cast. Too bad he wasn't as aware of manipulation when it came to Gay. Well, he was a grown man and hardly a victim. If he chose to be with Gay, he chose to be with Gay, period. Dave sat down.

"I thought it would be wise to tell you my philosophy so that there will be no confusion," Mike said, his eyes shifting from face to face so that there was no question he was addressing each of them. "Some changes will be made. To begin with, there has to be a change in attitude." The others shared glances.

"I've been observing you for only an hour and already

I can see that there is a definite caste system here," he continued, his eyes again fixing on each person in the room. Kate was glad to see her colleagues flinch uncomfortably. "Now we're here to do our work, not to rule over tiny private kingdoms. Do I make myself understood? The condescending, superior air used in this office has to go. For instance, all instructions to your subordinates are to be given in a clear and careful manner. Continue your explanation until you are sure you are understood."

"What if the person lacks the intelligence to understand?" Gay asked.

"Then they shouldn't have been hired in the first place and will be weeded out accordingly. But before the weeding," Mike added pointedly, "they are to come to see me. As a matter of fact, anyone with a problem is to come to see me as the first order of business."

Kate looked at him, surprised. Did he mean that?

"But what about hierarchy?" Dave sputtered. "They have to go to their supervisors first, then the unit leader, then—"

Mike cut through all this verbiage. "Desperate times deserve desperate measures, and this, by all indications, is a desperate time. This red tape is what's killing you in the first place. You have no communications system. You have no idea what your employees are thinking."

"Kate keeps us informed of that," Gay said dryly.

"Well, we need more of that," Mike said decisively, which made Gay smile in Kate's direction. How quickly she changed her colors.

"Well, yes, of course, we're interested in what they have to say, but you'll be inundated all day long. You won't be able to do your own work," Gay said, her eyes warm and sympathetic.

"That *is* my work," Mike told her flatly. Flustered finally, Gay moved back from the edge of the seat where she had been eagerly perched.

"The problem," Mike continued, "as I see it is that there is no company pride. And what is there to be proud of? Employees are treated like parts of a machine. There's no human component. It's difficult to feel pride in a company that dehumanizes you."

"We're no different from any other insurance company," Dave said defensively.

"Well, I want us to be," Mike said simply. "I want to foster a good atmosphere. Many businesses do use this philosophy, and it works. They make an employee feel like a vital part of the company," he continued. "Not just a worker but a person with intelligence whose opinion will be listened to. I'm here to listen.

"That's all for now," he finished. "I'll be getting to the others during the course of the day—I intend to hold a general meeting."

Which he did, later that morning. The entire office listened to the same speech he had given Kate and the others earlier. By the looks on their faces, a lot of people appeared heartened and hopeful. Well, Mike talked a good show, Kate thought, but whether things would actually change remained to be seen.

At lunch she returned to her car to study her lines. It was a warm day and she had the windows rolled down. Munching on a ham sandwich, she read several lines, closing her eyes as she tried to get the right inflections.

"Still working on that extracurricular reading?" a voice asked her.

Her eyes flew open to find Mike crouching down to the level of her open car window.

"Do you always work so hard, even at lunch?" he pressed when she made no response.

"Always," she replied.

"Good. I like that in a person," he told her, making no move to rise.

"Did you mean what you said this morning?" she found herself asking, her eyes dancing over the bronzed planes of his face. With his face so close to hers, she felt a compelling urge to throw her arms about his neck and pull him closer. She tried to detach herself and managed to do so with difficulty.

"I always mean everything I say," he said simply, smiling.

Kate looked at him carefully. He was still crouched by the window. "You must be uncomfortable," was all she could think of to say.

"I'm not. Are you?" He cocked his dark head slightly.

She raised an eyebrow. "No," she lied.

"Then why the cold shoulder?" he asked. "I thought you would approve of my office policies."

"Talk is cheap," she said. "I'd rather see some action."

His grin widened. "If it's action you want," he began invitingly, "come to dinner with me."

"I wasn't talking about that sort of action," Kate said, trying to sound businesslike. But her smile betrayed her. He had a way of drawing her out.

"A pity. I was," he said, his eyes twinkling merrily. "Dinner?" he repeated.

But that was out. She had rehearsal again tonight. She shook her head.

"Strictly business?" he prodded. "Expense account, even?"

"I really am busy," she said. "But I'm free for breakfast." Her response surprised her more than it did him. Well, she'd never find out what he was up to if she kept clear of him, she rationalized, determined not to admit she was getting excited at the mere thought of being alone with him.

"Breakfast it is," he said. "I'll meet you here in the parking lot at seven. Right now we'd better go in. Can't set a bad example for the others, can we?" He rose and opened the door of her car.

She slid out with difficulty—her legs were long and the driver's pit of the little Porsche was deep—and her performance was not wasted on Mike as his eyes slowly raked the length of her body. As she stood, he took her hand. Just the touch of his skin sent electrical shock waves through her. He must have felt them too. Anyway, he did not release her immediately.

"I think I can manage from here," she snapped, flustered. She shook her hand free.

"I'm sure you can," he murmured.

Throughout rehearsal that night Kate found his seductive, captivating eyes and handsome face flitting into her thoughts. Her mind focused on little else.

"Where are you tonight?" screamed Sam Jakes. The director was a short man who made up for that in sheer volume of voice. "That's the second time you've missed your damn line!"

Startled, Kate ran her hand through her hair, brushing the smooth blond strands from her face. "I'm sorry," she apologized. "It's just that I have things on my mind."

"Like the failure of this play?" he shot back.

All was still around them as the other players held their breaths. "It won't happen again," Kate promised.

"It had better not. All right, from the beginning of the scene. Take it again," Jakes commanded.

Unbidden, Mike's image returned. More careful this time, Kate managed to keep her performance intact. But, uncharacteristically, she was relieved when the rehearsal was over.

"You pulled that one together, Kate," her co-star said heartily as he walked off to collect his belongings and go home.

Kate was gratified, but she didn't dwell on the praise. She was too preoccupied with trying to sort out the confusion that her life was rapidly becoming. And she had to admit that, as untrustworthy as he seemed romantically, and as much as he could infuriate her at times, she was rapidly becoming captivated by a tall, dark, mysterious stranger who did things to her body and mind that she had heretofore only dreamed about.

Yet she knew little about him, beyond that his glance could reduce her to putty. Common sense warned her once again that to follow her desires would be sheer folly. At the very least she was asking for heartache. He would be gone as soon as the office problems were resolved. At the worst she could probably lose her job, and her pride made that possibility odious. To lose it fighting over a principle, such as a cost-of-living raise, was one thing. To lose it because she gave in and indulged in a romance was quite another.

Thoughtfully Kate drove home. Breakfast, she decided, would remain on the plane of business, and that was that. By the time she wheeled her Porsche into the garage, her mind felt freer. Michael Fleming was a temporary part of her workaday world, nothing more.

Appearing at the parking lot the next morning a scarce moment after Kate drove in, Mike approached her looking far better than any man had a right to. Kate noted this calmly as she climbed out of her car and into Mike's.

He headed for a quaint restaurant about two miles down the road. It was nearly empty. Still, he asked for a booth in the far corner.

"I like being alone with you," he explained.

Kate ignored the waitress's envious look and tried to ignore Mike's provocative comment, which wasn't easy. They were now alone with each other and their menus.

"Just coffee for me," Kate said crisply.

"Is that how you keep your figure?" he asked, regarding her slowly.

She was wearing a sleeveless green dress with a round neckline and a tiny white collar. The dress nipped in at the waist, accenting its smallness and emphasizing the fullness of her breasts. But when his eyes took possession of her, she felt suddenly naked.

"I don't like to overindulge," she told him. "Breakfast sits rather heavily in the morning—especially when there's all that work to face."

He smiled in response, and the smile was easy. She was surprised to realize that she almost felt relaxed. The waitress returned for their order.

Handing in his menu, Mike turned to Kate. "You really are dedicated, aren't you?" She merely shrugged. "Why?" he pursued.

"I don't believe in doing things in half measures," she replied honestly.

"Good," he said huskily, his tone seeming inappropriate to the subject at hand. She realized he had taken her hand. Oh damn, she thought. Yet as she gazed into his warm eyes, she was powerless to withdraw it.

For a moment Mike said nothing, simply holding her gaze. "You're far too pretty to be buried in insurance, you know."

"I'm not buried," she snapped, pulling her hand back at last. "I've got a respectable position and I'm in charge of a lot of people. That didn't come easy."

"And you've made some enemies along the way. If you were merely ambitious, you wouldn't have offended your superiors. You wouldn't have done things like circulate that petition."

"I'm not 'merely ambitious.' I'm interested in advancing but only in doing it honorably. I don't like what's going on here, and I don't care if Dave says it happens everywhere else. *I'm* not everywhere else. I'm here— part of this office—and I want to make it a good place to work." She looked at him, wondering what he thought of all this. "I suppose that sounds naive and idealistic."

"No," he said with a smile, shaking his head. "The employees certainly don't think so. They apparently trust you a great deal."

Kate shrugged. "I don't treat them the way the others do. I don't pretend to be better than they are."

Mike nodded his approval. Again she noted he had a way of drawing her out, making her relax. It was surprising how easy it was to talk to him.

"You know," he said finally, allowing his fingers to graze her face lightly, "I said you were pretty before, but I was wrong. You're beautiful. Especially when you're angry."

Kate flushed. "I *am* angry," she snapped, pulling back, "and not just about the office. *You* make me angry. You're far too—too personal!" She stopped, aware that she had talked a great deal and that Mike had cleverly drawn her out. Was he just curious, or was there something more to it? She almost wished she had never overheard that phone conversation. It made her constantly suspicious. But the fact was, she had.

"You make me feel personal," he said quietly.

She looked at him carefully, at the vast greenness of eyes that engulfed her with their magic. Somehow her suspicions, the situation with Gay, all seemed less vital. Another emotion was struggling hard to surface.

Mike put his hands on her shoulders and leaned forward across the table. Almost involuntarily Kate leaned forward, too. The look in his eyes made her melt. It said nothing about Icon Assurance, and everything about what was happening between them. Kate felt herself being pulled closer. Heat began to radiate through every part of her, starting in the center of her being and pouring out the corners. Leaning forward farther still, Mike cupped her chin in his left hand and brought her toward him. Ever so lightly he kissed her ripe, waiting mouth.

The kiss, soft and touching, lingered on her lips a long while. Kate knew Mike wished they weren't in a public place. She could read it in his eyes. And she could read it in her own soul. She pulled back, taking in her breath sharply.

"Just what do you think you're doing?" she said, trying to steady her breathing. "What about the office situation?" she reminded him, aware of the fact that the waitress was watching them from the far corner of the counter. "I thought our relationship was to remain strictly professional."

Mike laughed. "I can find you very attractive, Kate, and still be concerned about office affairs. I'm not a one-dimensional character, given over merely to lust."

She stiffened. "Is that what that was?"

He gazed at her face, as if trying to make up his mind about her. "You were there, too. What did you think? Was that pure animal lust?"

Evasively she looked away. He flustered her. As she reached for her purse, it fell open on the seat between them, and the contents of the bag spilled out, exposing a small tight roll of bills secured by a rubber band. The denomination of the outer bill was fifty.

Mike picked up the roll and looked at it closely. Suddenly serious, he stared at Kate. The expression in his eyes gave her a chill. "Carrying around your nest egg?"

He continued to hold her eyes with his. For the first time the intense green gaze did not hold a sexual promise. Instead it was as cold as steel.

Puzzled by the intensity of his reaction, Kate held out her hand for the roll. But Mike didn't offer to return it. Clearly he wanted an explanation first.

Kate felt indignant. Yet his attitude unnerved her, and in the end she merely stammered, "It's not mine."

"Oh? Robbing the rich to give to the poor?"

His tone was troubling too, not at all his usual bantering tease. Just what was he implying? She prided herself on the speed of her rejoinders—witty, she hoped. But suddenly she found herself with nothing at all to say. "One more guess and your turn is up," she said at last, trying for glibness and failing.

"You tell me," he suggested coldly.

She bristled. So he *was* accusing her of something, grilling her. "It belongs to Gladys," she said frostily.

She probably shouldn't have answered at all. He really had his nerve. Stiffly she extended her hand.

"Rather high for a housekeeper's pay," was his comment as he relinquished the money and watched her put it away.

"It's her winnings," Kate clarified grudgingly. "She finally won. She asked me to deposit it for her during lunch—to save her the trip into town."

"So you're running her errands now?"

"Along with her winnings," Kate responded, an icy edge to her voice, "she also came back with a king-size cold, so I volunteered to be her errand girl for a change. Anything else you want to know?"

"No," he said slowly, as if debating whether to believe her.

Kate looked at the golden-faced watch on her left wrist. "It's time to get back," she said.

Mike made no comment, only nodded. Taking out his wallet, he removed several bills and left them on the table. "Let's go to work," he said finally.

The bright splash of daylight outside hurt Kate's eyes as she followed him into the parking lot. The ride back to the office was stiffly silent. Once they were inside the Icon building, she went to her desk and he to his office.

But despite her confusion and anger, the memory of his kiss stayed with her for a long time.

Things had begun to pick up in the office. As he had promised, Mike did not disappear whenever someone wanted to talk to him. Word quickly spread that the new office manager did not just nod his head, staring off into oblivion the way his predecessor had, making no comments and leaving the distraught person with no hope. Mike had the ability to listen sympathetically and offer constructive comments. He wasted no time in looking into matters. Supervisors were made to feel that they were to be mentors and that their titles did not exclude them from sharing the work load.

Subtle changes began taking place. Mike had the rented desks that were on the verge of falling apart replaced with desks that Icon was made to purchase. Soon everyone was properly supplied rather than being forced to borrow necessary books and tools from each other. All complaints about the office were taken into consideration and acted upon immediately. Pride in the office had begun to set in.

At the end of the second week Mike held a small buffet lunch as a reward for the effort he had seen put out. But through all this he remained as much of a mystery to Kate as ever.

More than once she found herself wondering what he had been like when he was in his twenties and how he had gotten to where he was now. She knew from articles in the monthly newsletter that was now making the rounds again—this time being read almost like fan magazine articles by the women employees—that he had been voted Icon's Young Man of the Year three times in a row. Obviously he was an asset to the company. His techniques might be unorthodox by business standards, but they worked. Icon's president seemed to appreciate vastly having Mike "on his team," if one was to believe the articles.

But the information they divulged only told Kate about Michael Fleming, company man. They said nothing about Michael Fleming, private citizen, and she found herself desperately wanting to know more about him, even while she told herself not to get more emotionally involved than she was.

She spent much of her time watching him. She noted that he was systematically taking people into his office for long, solitary conferences. To her relief, Gay wasn't the only one closeted with him, and Kate had watched

him take both Milt and Dave to lunch on different oc-
casions. And each morning he would disappear into his
office with another pile of personnel files. Something
was definitely up.

But even knowing this, Kate couldn't help being jealous each time she saw Gay with Mike. Almost a week
had passed, and he hadn't sought out Kate's company
again. It bothered her. But late rehearsals were being
held six nights a week now, and she had other activities
to occupy her mind.

Still, even she had to admit that her efforts to remain
emotionally aloof had failed. Oh, why couldn't he look
like Dave Martin or Al Baines? Why did he have to be
so devastatingly attractive, so beguilingly charming? So
damn sexy, she thought, pursing her lips.

Then, the following Monday, Kate was summoned to
Mike's office.

"Kate," he said after she closed the door, "I have a
problem."

She watched the tall figure in the navy suit as he rose
and pulled forth a large portfolio from a side cabinet.
He placed it in front of her. In it were four separate books
on policy description. She felt his nearness as he spread
papers to her left. Hold me, her mind begged. Sternly
she clamped a tight lid on such thoughts.

Mike was all business now, or at least his voice was.
His eyes said other, more disturbing things to her.

"Recognize this?" he asked, taking a seat next to her
on the other side of his desk, his fingers touching her
lightly, tantalizingly.

She picked up one of the booklets. "It's the Casbah
account," she said, flipping through the pages. The Casbah hotel in Las Vegas was one of the western region's
largest accounts.

Mike nodded. "They're about to pull their business
away from Icon," he said. "They were being handled by
the Salt Lake office. You see, Carson City isn't the only

branch having problems." He smiled. "Anyway," he continued, "it seems that whenever anyone from personnel called Salt Lake, they got a royal runaround. No one had any answers. The files they asked for were never in, and the claims weren't being processed. Worse, whenever the Casbah people asked to speak to any of the office officials, they were told that the person was either unavailable, out of the office, or on another line. Few if any calls were ever returned. I don't have to tell you that this is a multimillion-dollar account, and it's going to cause a big gap in Icon's treasury if it goes."

"So it's being transferred here?" Kate asked, surprised.

"Lock, stock, and barrel—as a vote of confidence in my ability, I suppose," he said. His eyes narrowed as his gaze took in only her. "And it's going to you." Even when he was speaking about business, she felt as if every word was an intimate pronouncement. If this was a campaign to undermine her sensibilities, it was working, she thought ruefully.

Her head began to ache. "Did you think of using Gay?" she couldn't help but ask.

"No, I didn't," he said, momentarily avoiding her eyes. "You're the one to handle it. You're fast and efficient. Without your efforts, we haven't got a prayer. I think so and Asherton thinks so."

"Asherton?" she echoed, surprised.

Mike laughed. "He may think of you as a pain in his—side, shall we say," he amended politely, "but he seems to know your worth, and in the long run he knows he can count on you."

"He has a funny way of showing it," Kate muttered, already beginning to thumb through the few folders that Mike had brought out for her. She sighed. "Okay, when do I start?"

"Right away," he told her. "We have a meeting in five days with three of their representatives who are flying up to the conference area. They have a whole list of grievances they want to go over."

"Do I get to see the grievances ahead of time?" she asked.

"That's my girl," Mike said, pulling out a three-page list from his inner pocket.

Kate studied the list, hiding behind the paper to keep from looking at Mike. He had called her his girl. It was only a remark, of course, but oh, how she loved the sound of it.

Get hold of yourself, Kate. You're only buying trouble, she warned herself.

"Okay, bring on the claims," she said, rising.

Her desk was soon surrounded with brown boxes of folders, both with and without claims attached. Three bewildered file girls sat on the floor Indian-fashion, trying to uncover the mysterious folders that went with the names on the typed lists they held.

Tackling the job on her own, Kate spent the rest of the day going over the policy coverage documents and rereading the complaints that had come in. Meticulously she went over each of the folders the women had pulled for her, making notes and correcting the errors. She was nowhere near finished by quitting time, but she dashed out the door, barely making rehearsal.

The following day was spent in much the same fashion. She tried to field questions from her own people while continuing to untangle the vast web that had been willed to her by the negligent Salt Lake office. The predominant problem, she discovered, was that no one seemed to have wanted to process anything. Claims with memos questioning them were stapled to the inside left covers, and hardly any payments had been made to the group, which had been with Icon almost a year and regretted every moment of it, according to the correspondence.

After having come in early and given up lunch for four days, Kate began to see daylight.

That same day she watched Gay corner Mike by the water cooler and, eyelashes fluttering and eyes sincere, invite him out to lunch to discuss some problems she was having with her accounts. To Kate's chagrin, Mike smiled down into the woman's tip-tilted eyes and agreed— eagerly, Kate thought—to go. Others noticed, too. By the end of the week it was being whispered about that an office affair was in the offing.

Kate, trying to bite back her feelings, told herself she was lucky. There were a million reasons not to get involved with Mike; here was just one more. She turned her attention back to the claim form at hand, a feat requiring superhuman effort. She had the meeting tomorrow to think of.

Mike had an appointment scheduled for two o'clock that day and left right after lunch. He would not be back. As if by silent agreement, the others filed out between the hours of three and five, shutting off their machines and closing down their minds for the day. The last green light had gone off and Kate was still at her desk. Since rehearsal had been canceled for that day, she felt compelled to resolve the last of Casbah's problems before going home. She wanted everything to be ready the next day, with no last-minute surprises.

A call to Gladys informing her that she was working late brought no sympathy.

"You're working yourself to death," the woman chided her.

"Uh-huh. Don't wait up," Kate managed to get in amid the tirade.

"How long do you intend to stay there?"

"Until I'm finished, Gladys. Good night." With that Kate hung up, shaking her head.

Oh well, she thought, kicking off her high-heeled

sandals, Gladys meant well. She couldn't understand being dedicated to anything but show business. That was probably why her father had insisted she take Gladys on as a housekeeper. He was hoping the feisty woman would eventually win Kate over.

The air conditioning had shut down at five o'clock, emitting its last gutteral whoosh at three minutes to, and now, at seven, it was becoming very hot and stuffy. Kate kept promising herself that after the next claim she would go home. But several "next claims" went by and she was still there, her mind struggling, accompanied only by the green glow of the computer screen.

The janitor had come and gone, asking her to please lock the door behind her when she left, and now there was no sound except for the click of the keyboard machine when she finally managed to unscramble something well enough to feed it.

The sound of footsteps in the hallway penetrated her thoughts, and she raised her head to hear better, wondering who it was. The sound grew nearer. She knew there was a guard downstairs, but he did her precious little good up here. She also knew that the office had been vandalized a couple of times in the past two years, with the intruders taking a secretary's typewriter both times. Now the office was full of computers, almost all brand new. What an attractive haul that would make.

Kate got up and hid by the side of the first line of files, watching the far door open slowly. A tall figure entered. She caught her breath.

"What are you doing here?" she cried, her adrenaline settling down to be replaced by a quickening of her heart. Perhaps it was only her tired state, but Mike seemed unusually attractive tonight. His presence filled the room.

He looked at her. "More important, what arc *you* doing here? Do you realize it's almost nine o'clock?"

She shrugged, suddenly feeling the ache of all the

tense muscles in her back. "I lost track of time," she admitted, padding back to her desk in her bare feet.

"Wish you found me as fascinating as those claims," he said, and Kate tried not to react to his words in anything but a professional manner.

"You gave them to me," she pointed out, sitting down and slipping into her shoes.

"I didn't mean for you to kill yourself in the process," he replied.

"You're the second one who said that to me today," she told him, tired of being told what to do.

"Well, whoever else said it had good sense—more than you."

Tired, she bristled. "If I lack sense, why did you give the account to me?"

"Down, Kate. That's not the point. It's dangerous for a woman to be here alone late at night—especially such an attractive woman."

"I can take care of myself," she retorted, sniffing.

"By hiding behind a file bin?" he asked in an even voice.

"I know karate," she retorted coldly.

"Thanks for the warning," he replied. "Who taught you that?"

"One of my brothers," she said, offering no more information.

"How many do you have?"

"Three. Two older and a twin," she finally offered, seeing the continuing question in his eyes.

"You have a twin? You mean there's some guy who looks exactly like you?" he asked in surprise.

Kate smiled. "Not exactly."

"And no sister?" he resumed, sitting on her desk and looking down at her. She felt stifled and closed off with her back to the large window that looked down the deserted parking lot.

"None," she said, her eyes not leaving his.

He put a crooked finger beneath her chin, raising it to study her face.

"Too bad, although I do like having one of a kind," he said in his low, seductive voice.

Kate stood up, trembling at his nearness yet annoyed by his smugness. "You don't have anything," she said, taking up her purse, ready to leave.

"As you wish," he said. His voice caressed her like a velvet glove. Suddenly he was off the desk and enfolding her in his arms, his lips covering hers so quickly that she had no idea how it had even happened.

Her purse fell from her fingers as the kiss grew, drawing away her breath and her senses so rapidly that she felt dizzy. The tingling she had felt in the past at his nearness now rose in a deep crescendo, encircling her with music and bright colors as his lips impressed themselves upon hers, raising such excitement within her that she thought she couldn't bear it. Her knees felt weak, and were she not pressed against his body, she doubted she could have stood on her own.

Ever so gently his hands caressed her back, pressing her closer and closer to him, making her want to be even nearer, making her want him so fiercely that it frightened her. Yet caution intervened. Clearly Mike was involved in something, something Kate had yet to untangle. Until she knew exactly what it was—and how she fit into it— she intended to keep a clear head and act cautiously. And this meant keeping him at arm's length.

"You shouldn't have done that," she snapped, wishing she didn't sound as if she had just run the five-minute mile.

"Sure I should have," he said easily.

"You can't go around kissing every woman you see—"

"I don't," he assured her.

"—and thinking she's going to be grateful for your attention."

"I'm not asking for gratitude," he said. His sly smile disarmed her.

Kate threw up her hands. "I'm going home!" she cried, exasperated.

"Wait. Let me just get my papers and I'll walk you to your car," he called after her.

But she was already out the door, annoyed with herself for succumbing so easily. She pressed the elevator button and waited for the car to arrive. It did, and the doors closed just as Mike entered the hallway. Kate breathed a sigh of relief and leaned against the elevator door, her heart pounding. She had to get away quickly. Her angry tone to the contrary, she knew he was wearing her down fast—and so was her own desire. Oh, how she wanted him to hold her, to stoke the flames of the magic glow he had already lit inside her. Hurriedly she ran for the white Porsche that waited brightly in its lonely spot, silhouetted against the inky night.

The engine wouldn't turn over. It made a whining noise, but no matter how hard she pumped the gas and turned the key, she could coax no further response. She looked up to see Mike coming toward her, his steps deliberate and sure, unhurried.

"Got trouble?" he asked, leaning over to look in.

"Other than an amorous manager?" she said dryly.

He only laughed. "That's not a problem," he told her. "Need a lift?"

"No, I need this started."

"Won't find a garage open now," he told her. And it was true. The office, although it was a large, impressive complex, was totally isolated, located in the middle of nowhere. There was an empty field on either side of it. The small gas station two miles off had long since closed.

"Well?" she said expectantly. "You're a man."

"Glad you noticed."

"Fix it," she told him, gesturing at the engine.

But he shook his head. "I'm a man, not a garage mechanic. The most I can do is offer a lady in distress a ride home."

She gave a token look about but knew she had no options—unless she wanted to spend the night in the office. Against her better judgment, she stepped out of the car.

"That's better. Now you're acting sensibly. You shouldn't have run off that way. Karate or no karate," he added, regarding her as if he was amused. She knew he was laughing at her, and she didn't like it.

He held the door open for her and slid in behind the wheel. "My place or yours?" he asked.

"My place."

"Oh, good. I like your place better."

Kate's cheeks flushed. "You may be the home office's boy wonder, Michael Fleming, but you're not mine!"

"That's not what your kiss told me upstairs," he said mildly. She could hear the smile in his voice even though she wasn't looking at him.

"Do you read palms too?" she snapped.

"I'll read anything you want to show me."

"The only thing I want to show you is the door once you bring me home," she informed him, staring straight ahead into the night.

"Which door?" he asked in a husky voice, and Kate decided that it was better not to try for conversation.

They rode in silence. A few minutes later he turned to her and said, "So how does it look?"

"What?" she asked cautiously.

"The Casbah situation." He turned the car down a long road near where she lived.

"I think we'll be all right," she said, relaxing just a little. "I've managed to make a lot of payments in the last three days, and I think I've resolved at least the bulk of the problems to their satisfaction. But of course I can't be sure till we meet with them. Will you be there?"

"That's my job," he told her, pulling the car into her driveway. "At least for now. Besides, I wouldn't miss seing you in action." He brushed the thick hair from her cheek. "Any sort of action."

"Mike, don't start again," she implored. Quickly she got out of the car.

"I never stopped," he said, following her.

"Well, this is where I live," she muttered needlessly. They had reached the front door. "You can go home now," she added.

Mike didn't budge. "Oh now, my father taught me my job wasn't done until I escorted the lady into her house."

"What else did your father teach you?" she asked, fumbling for her key.

"Someday I'll show you," he promised softly into her hair, his breath warm and sweet.

Kate's stomach fluttered wildly. She bit deeply into her lip, but the feelings flooding her body did not subside.

CHAPTER
# *Five*

BEFORE SHE COULD recover, Mike had taken the key from her hand and unlocked the door.

She tried to squeeze past him. "Well, thank you," she said hesitantly.

"My father specifically said 'inside her door,'" Mike said, following her into the house. A small yellow glow coming from the kitchen was the only light against the darkness.

"What was your father, a gate-crasher?" Kate asked, wondering if Gladys was asleep. If so, she was as good as alone with Mike. Gladys could sleep through a train wreck.

"No, a very wise man," Mike said, cornering her against the door.

How did she get in this position, Kate wondered angrily. "Well," she said, struggling for calm. "I'd better get a good night's sleep if I'm to meet the lions of the Casbah tomorrow." She hoped that would make him release her. She felt the warmth of his body as he leaned forward.

He was making no move to go. "It's only nine-thirty," he told her, kissing the side of her neck. "I could have you in bed by ten." It sounded like a promise. Part of Kate really wanted to take him up on it. It was only her nagging uncertainty about his motives that kept her in check. Would he try to compromise her in order to fire her? It hardly seemed likely. Yet the home office had tried to defuse the office agitator once before. And how did Gay Ling fit into the picture?

"I'm going to bed alone," she said firmly, pushing him away.

Yet his strong hands found her shoulders again, and his lips discovered the other side of her neck. Small, sensuous kisses delighted her flesh as they traveled from shoulder to ear. She was powerless to stop him.

"Ever notice what the rest of that word is comprised of?" he whispered as the tip of his tongue caressed the outline of her ear. Heat surged through her. "'Lone' is part of 'lonely.' You're too beautiful to be lonely." His arms caressed her slowly, memorizing the curves of her figure as he pressed her closer and closer to him. His lips now covered hers and took her breath away with a dramatic thrust that swept aside all sense of reality. Kate no longer had any will of her own. Instead, she molded herself against him, her arms going about his neck, her fingers entangling themselves in his luxurious hair.

The light suddenly flooding the hallway broke like a glaring meteor into the abyss that surrounded her. Startled, Kate's head jerked up, her eyes blinking away the mist of passion.

Glady stood in the hall. She wore her green bathrobe, and rollers graced her tinted hair. The look of annoyance on her face abated once she had taken a good look at Mike.

"Oh, I'm sorry. I thought you were her boss, bringing her home," she stammered, her eyes obviously appreciating what they saw.

"I am," he told her graciously. "Michael Fleming, ma'am." He took her hand warmly.

For one brief moment Gladys seemed about to float away. "I can see why she wants to work overtime."

"Gladys!" Kate cried. The grin on Mike's face widened.

"Need any help at the office?" Gladys offered with a chuckle, circling him to check him out in detail.

"Gladys," Kate said a little more sharply. She glanced at Mike, but Gladys's obvious appraisal didn't seem to make him uncomfortable in the slightest.

"I'm going, I'm going," Gladys said, raising her hands defensively. "I can see when two people want to be alone." She began to shuffle back toward her room.

Alone. No, Kate didn't want to be alone with Mike right now. She was too tired to think clearly and too confused to resist. "Gladys, I want you to stay right here," Kate said, calling after the figure in the housecoat.

"Sure, kid, sure. Play hard to get—but don't let that one get away!" Gladys called over her shoulder and disappeared into her room, firmly shutting the door behind her.

"So that's Gladys," Mike said, his tone registering amusement.

"None other," Kate said ruefully. She flipped on the brass lamp on the end table. The light it cast was warm and romantic.

"I think she's my father's spy," Kate told him. "He didn't think his little girl could take care of herself, I suppose."

"I take it that means he never took the time to get to know you," Mike said. He sat down on the sofa.

Kate glared at him. "I thought you were going home."

"Funny, I didn't think that." He grinned. "Besides, if I don't stay a little while, Gladys will be awfully disappointed."

"I'll explain it to her," Kate said. She sat down on the far edge of the sofa, determined not to tumble into his arms.

"I can't reach you," Mike said, noting the distance between them.

"I was hoping that would be the case," Kate replied, not moving.

"Ah, well, if the mountain won't come to Muhammad..." He slid over until he was barely inches from her.

"I really think you should go."

"Then you're outvoted." Kate looked at him, puzzled. "Gladys and I think I should stay," he clarified, putting his arm around her shoulders. "What are you afraid of?" he asked softly.

There was that smugness again. "Don't flatter yourself. I don't understand you, that's all."

"Not much to understand," Mike said easily, his eyes touching her face as intimately as if his hand had done it. "I'm just a plain, simple guy." He moved still closer.

"And if I believe that, there's this bridge you want to sell me, right?" she asked drolly.

He laughed. "You certainly are a cautious one."

"I've learned to be," she told him crisply, looking down at her hands.

"Tell me about him," Mike said, his voice lowering slightly. He sounded so sincere, so interested, that she felt almost compelled to confide in him about her marriage. Well, why not? Let him see just why she hated dishonesty and deception.

"'Him' was a magnificent creature who swept me off my feet with the sweetest words God ever manufactured on the tongue of a snake," she said simply. "But while my young, palpitating heart was beating so hard in my ears, I missed catching some very obvious signs until after I said 'I do.'"

"Obvious signs?" Mike repeated, his brow furrowing.

Kate shrugged. "He was using me. My father—" she hesitated a moment and decided against telling Mike who her father really was. Mike wasn't the only one with a secret. But hers was only meant to protect her against further hurt, she rationalized quickly. It didn't harm anyone. "My father is a well-to-do businessman, and Ryan— my ex—wanted Dad to help him further his career ambitions. I was just a stepping stone," she concluded, looking up at Mike, her eyes bright, slightly defensive. "End of little tragedy. But you can see why I hate deception, can't you?" she asked pointedly, watching his face.

He didn't flinch. A real pro, she thought with annoyance.

"I certainly can," Mike said, "but I wouldn't let what happened between you and this Ryan character color your relationships with other men."

She was aware of the pressure of his thigh against hers. She could smell his cologne, and the mere scent of it aroused her. "Any particular men?" She hoped her tone was sarcastic.

"One very likely candidate does pop up." His voice was scarcely louder than a whisper. His fingers played with the nape of her neck, sending shivers up and down her spine.

This is crazy, she tried to tell herself as she sank against his chest. Nothing was going to come of it. For all she knew, he wasn't even who he said he was.

"Who are you?" she asked suddenly.

Surprised, Mike looked at her. "Want to see my driver's license?" he offered.

"No."

"My resumé?" he ventured.

"No." He wouldn't be serious, darn him.

"I could strip down to my underwear and have you inspect me . . ." he suggested with a twinkle in his eye.

"I'll pass, thank you." But the image of Mike with little on did delicious things to her mind. A warm smile tugged at the corners of her lips, but she fought it back.

It was taking more and more effort to keep a clear mind. But Kate was stubborn. "I want answers," she said.

Mike sighed, releasing her. "Okay, I'm Michael Fleming, born at a young age to—"

"Your charm won't work this time," Kate told him. "Not on me."

"Oh." He sounded disappointed. "And I thought I was doing so well . . ."

Kate opened her mouth to continue her line of questioning, but Mike kissed her so deeply that her words were lost. She was stunned. This was no tender kiss. This was a hungry demand. For a brief moment she gave herself up to the surging wave of excitement with her.

Deftly Mike's strong, sure fingers went beneath the red blazer she was wearing. Gently they fondled the outline of her breasts, straining against the crisp ruffled white blouse. She felt another, more intense wave of heat as he began to unbutton the blouse, searching for the soft flesh beneath it. Ever so gently his hand stroked the planes above her breasts, going lower and lower until it slipped inside the silky material of her bra and cupped one firm breast, massaging it over and over.

A low moan escaped her lips as her breath grew shorter and shorter. Stop him, stop him now, her mind urged, before it's too late. But she really didn't want to give up the delicious feeling that cascaded through her veins. Not yet.

You must, her mind urged.

With a control she didn't know she had, Kate managed to push him back. "I'm not a philosophy major," she said. She was trying hard not to gasp for air.

"What?" Mike asked.

"When I talk about honesty and deception, I'm not just idly expounding," she snapped. She sat up and straightened her clothing. "I've heard the rumors about you and Gay Ling. I want you to know I don't care that you choose to see both of us," she lied. Mike seemed to be intrigued by this. "What I do mind is dishonesty," she continued. "Don't pretend you're nuts about me if I'm just one of two. Or many. Give me a *little* credit."

"I'm only trying to promote good working relations with Gay," he said casually.

"You're trying to do more than that."

He paused, as if thinking something over. "Smart lady," he commented finally.

"So my father told me." She took a deep breath. "What is it you're investigating?"

The word seemed to startle him. "What makes you think I'm investigating anything?"

"Your first morning in the office, I picked up the phone by accident." She looked at him intently, but he merely gave a slow nod. "How am I involved in this?" she asked bluntly.

"You're not," he said. "Not any more. Not in the investigation, at any rate. You can be as involved with me as you want," he added, his eyes mischievous. But they held a hint of seriousness, too. Kate could see that she had unsettled him.

"If I'm no longer a suspect in whatever you're investigating, tell me about it," she urged.

"I can't," he said simply, spreading his hands for emphasis.

She peered into his eyes. "You don't trust me?"

"Right now I'm not in a position to trust anyone."

His words carved a chasm between them, cutting through any intimacy. If he trusted her, things would be different. Perhaps she should be grateful for this—but she wasn't. "Neither am I," she said, rising. "It's getting late." At just that moment the clock at the entrance chimed ten. Lucky, she thought.

"Even Cinderella had till twelve," Mike countered quickly when the chimes had ceased.

Kate was not amused. "Cinderella didn't have to field slings and arrows from the Casbah representatives in the morning," she said tightly.

He stood stiffly, his tension apparent in his stance. "Did you tell anyone else about the phone call?" Kate shook her head. Mike's relief was apparent. "Good," he said.

He gripped her shoulders. "Perhaps you have a point. After all, I'm supposed to be revitalizing your office. I'm not exactly doing that by keeping my best worker up until the wee hours of the morning." He cupped her face in his hands. His long, loving kiss thrilled Kate down to her fingertips.

"I'll come by and pick you up tomorrow morning," he said when he released her.

"I'm perfectly able to drive myself in," she protested, her heart pounding.

"Not even you can do that without a car," he pointed out.

Her car! She had forgotten all about it. Suddenly she was embarrassed. Surely he must know that he made her forget everything else around her. "All right, I'll be ready at six-thirty," she told him.

He touched her face fondly. "I'm ready anytime," he said, and with that, he turned to let himself out the door. With a final wave, he was gone.

Kate sighed, leaning against the closed door. Never had she met a man who stirred her to such heights. But what was Mike Fleming really after? How could she trust a man who was so secretive?

"Now *that's* the man you need," Gladys said, appearing suddenly in her doorway as Kate prepared to go off to bed.

"Eavesdropping again?" Kate demanded, her cheeks growing hot.

Gladys held up her hands in innocent protest. "Just listening for the sound of a door. I was hoping to hear one other than the front door," she commented dryly.

"Go to bed, Gladys," Kate said wearily. "It's late."

"Later than you think," the housekeeper called after her.

"There's more involved than you know, Gladys," Kate muttered as she went off to her room. If only it were so simple. For a while she, too, had imagined she would not be alone in bed tonight. But she couldn't give herself up to passion while there were unanswered questions between them. Perhaps it was unrealistic to think that Mike would try to entrap her. It was hard for her to believe he would deliberately try to get her fired—or otherwise "defuse" her. On the other hand, this investigation of his worried her, and his refusal to confide in her worried her even more. And then there was the nagging question of Gay. He'd said he was trying to promote good working relations with Gay. And yet . . . some sixth sense told her there was more to it than that. His inability to play it straight with her, to confide in her, was keeping them at arm's length. It was his own fault, she told herself. She had good reason to be wary.

Of course, principles don't keep you warm at night, she reminded herself as she stirred restlessly in bed. Sometimes, Kate Lonigan, you're your own worst enemy. She snapped off the bedside light.

Kate dressed with care the next morning, donning a pale blue linen suit with a trim mocha color blouse. She bound her hair up neatly on top of her head, using a single clip, then stood back before her mirror, gauging the effect. The new hairstyle gave her a more sophisticated air, she decided.

"Not bad, not bad," Gladys said, her eyes still puffy

from sleep as she got Kate her morning coffee. "But your skirt should be higher," she said, pointing to the hemline. "You've got a great set of legs. Show them off. Use everything you've got."

"Gladys, I'm going to *work*," Kate said, nibbling at the single piece of toast on her plate. Gladys had forgotten to butter it again. "I'm not setting a trap for a man," she said, adding as an afterthought, "Especially not Michael Fleming."

"Then you're crazy," Gladys pronounced, picking up a coffee cup and seating herself next to Kate at the breakfast table. "How you can sit there and tell me you'd let a man that good-looking get away is beyond me." She shook her curler-capped head to and fro.

Kate let her go on for a bit as she watched the early-morning sun peek into the kitchen, bathing it in warm rays. Finally she could take it no longer.

"Looks aren't everything, Gladys," she snapped. Actually she was a little put out that she could be read so easily.

"No," Gladys agreed, wagging a finger. "But it's just as simple to fall in love with a guy who's easy on the eyes as one who's not." The doorbell rang. "That him?" Her face showed her eagerness.

"I suppose so," Kate replied. Who else would be ringing her bell at six-thirty in the morning? A sudden nervousness took hold of her. She thought, This is absurd. After all, I took the role in *Rain* without batting an eye. This was no time to lose her cool.

"Knock 'im dead, kid," Gladys said and shuffled out of the room with such speed that Kate looked after her in surprise.

"Hello, Kate," Mike said, peering into the room behind her. "My cheering section asleep?"

Kate grabbed up her briefcase and shoulder bag from the hall table, stuffing in the folder she had carried to the door. "No, she decided to clear a path for you in case you had something other than business on your mind."

"I'm beginning to like that lady," he said, taking Kate's elbow as he escorted her toward the door.

Kate chose not to answer that. The drive to the office passed in silence. As they pulled into the parking lot, she saw they were the first—and only—car there. She looked about in surprise. Where was the Porsche?

"I had a mechanic tow your car away last night," he told her. "He's seeing what he can do for it this morning."

"But I have the key," she protested.

He gave her a wicked grin. "He said he didn't need a key to start the engine."

She looked aghast as he opened the door to let her out. "You let some hood take my car?" she cried.

"Calm yourself, Katie. He comes with a good reputation. I wouldn't have entrusted your car to just anyone," he promised. "Hmmm, you smell good. And your hair looks nice that way."

"I thought packaging was important today," she said offhandedly. In truth she was thrilled that he had noticed.

"I'm sure they won't hear a word you're saying. Not if they're men," he said as they walked onto their floor. He took out his key and unlocked the door.

"But I want them to hear me," Kate said. "I didn't spend four days working hard just to charm them with my appearance. If that was the case, you could have given the account to Gay." Whoops, she thought. Her jealousy was showing—again!

"No, I couldn't," he replied, following her to her desk. "Gay isn't nearly as capable at her job as you are."

"You certainly do know how to turn a phrase, don't you?" Kate asked, smiling at him.

"With the right people," he said with a wink. "Meeting's at ten. Will you be ready at nine-thirty?"

"I've never been late for anything in my life," she informed him proudly.

"Another sterling quality," he told her. "Katie, my love, where have you *been* all my life?"

"Learning to fend off wolves," she told him, batting her eyes.

"Ah, you wound me," he said, placing a hand over his heart.

Behind them, a few of the claims adjusters had begun to file in.

"Don't forget your notes," Mike said. Kate saw that his face had grown serious once again.

Back to work, she thought.

Gay surprised Kate by arriving at seven-thirty and turning her attention to work within the first hour. To be fair, Kate had noticed that every so often Gay did apply herself.

Soon, however, Kate was too besieged with questions from her unit and with phone calls to give the situation much thought. In what seemed like no time at all, Mike appeared, casting a long shadow over her work.

"Ready?" he asked.

"Ready," she replied, shutting off her computer and taking her purse from the bottom drawer. Her briefcase was already out on her desk.

She responded to the pressure of his hand as he placed it lightly against her shoulder and ushered her from the office. Warm flushes rose inside her as she yearned for closer contact. What was there about this man that his slightest touch chased all sensible thoughts from her mind? She looked up at his face, so teasingly close to her as he shut the door behind her. She knew he sensed her thoughts; it was written in his eyes. It made her feel very vulnerable, and she drew up to her full height, assuming what she hoped was a businesslike stance as they entered the parking lot. He paced in a determined way toward the car, unresponsive to her silent plea for an added gesture, a touch. To be swept into his arms...

# CHAPTER
# *Six*

ONCE THEY WERE alone in the car, Mike seemed more relaxed, more sensual. How could he turn off and on like that? And if he could, could she believe anything he said? He was a better actor than many people she knew. Was he just amusing himself with her?

"Nervous?" he asked.

She wasn't sure whether he was referring to the Casbah account or what was passing between them. But she knew the best answer to both: a firm "No."

"Good," he said, patting her knee ever so gently. His fingers left behind a heated imprint on her stockinged leg.

He knew exactly what he was doing to her. Well, if this was a test to see if she'd melt at his touch, she'd show him. For the duration of their drive Kate kept up a steady flow of conversation. All of it was in direct reference to the Casbah account.

Icon's new conference hall was located in the Universal Savings & Loan building in the heart of Carson City. Participants in meetings that Icon held there were provided with a variety of restaurants and shows to occupy their free hours. Those who were so inclined could take an Icon-sponsored tour to the house where Mark Twain had lived. All this, Kate knew, was to put people in a jovial mood for the meetings.

But the entourage from Casbah looked far from jovial. Kate felt that the two women as well as the tall, thin man they flanked were watching her as she entered in front of Mike. She wished she felt as cheerfully confident as Mike appeared. But she mustered her best smile as she nodded at the group, then slid into her seat at the table facing them. The three people looked tailor-made for the job of administrating health insurance—dry, humorless, and tough.

"Hello, Kate," Asherton said, rising from his place at the head of the conference table. She tried not to show her surprise as the vice-president of the western region took her hand warmly and shook it. She knew this was only a show for the three solemn people who faced her. "This is Kate Lonigan," Asherton told them. The three viewed her critically but without comment. "She's done a terrific job in alleviating your, ah, difficulties."

Kate nodded at the group and reseated herself.

"And this is Michael J. Fleming," Asherton said proudly. The name obviously meant nothing to the other people present there. "Now that he's handling things, you'll really see some action," Asherton promised.

The Casbah contingent looked as though they doubted it. They were introduced in turn. Once the social amenities were out of the way, war was declared, with Asherton sitting in as mediator. Sympathetically, he expressed concern over each grievance raised by the personnel director or his two assistants. Kate felt like Daniel in the lion's den, but continued to listen patiently.

One of the two women took the main offensive, pointing out claim upon unprocessed claim. She took out copies of memos that ran in windy circles and made no sense, serving only to confuse the recipient. The stack grew quite high. Finally she folded her arms before herself and waited. It was Kate's turn. Round two, she thought.

For every name the woman had raised, Kate had an answer. At first she knew the Las Vegas group thought she was merely being clever by repeating the name and then rendering an immediate solution. But when this continued name after name, case after case, the faces on the Casbah delegation changed. Kate was able to cite the specific file and all the relevant information and could explain precisely what had been done—emphasizing the word "done"—to solve the dilemma and render payment.

"As a matter of fact," she said, opening her briefcase, "I have about fifty payment checks here with me."

Asherton looked on in surprise as Kate drew out a stack of blue checks. It was totally unprecedented for a second assistant actually to handle checks. Hand-carrying checks was strictly the province of the office manager.

Kate caught Mike's look. "Desperate times . . ." she quoted his words of several weeks ago.

He smiled his support.

Asherton sputtered but kept up his facade, since the Casbah delegation looked surprised—and definitely pleased—by her action.

"I realize that this does little to make up for the time your employees have been waiting for their money," she finished. "But I hope you'll assure them that from now on claims will be processed promptly. And phone calls—not letters—will be used to discuss any problems. I look forward to working closely with the two of you." She nodded to the two women, who were allowing themselves just a hint of a smile.

"Then you'll be doing the claims yourself?" one of them pressed. She had been introduced as Amy Lessing, a name Kate knew well from the correspondence.

"Yes," Kate assured her. "If not directly, then I'll be overseeing the operation. And I can *always* be reached." This was in reference to the fact that the Salt Lake people had rarely taken any of the phone calls Amy had placed. "The problems you had in the past were unfortunate, but I hope you don't write off the entire company because of the mistakes made by one office. Some of us really do care about the people on the other end of those forms." She glanced at Asherton but couldn't read his expression. Finally he nodded.

The Casbah personnel director cleared his throat. "Well, that sounds rather refreshing. But only time will tell if the young woman means her words."

"The young woman always means her words," Mike interrupted.

His support came spontaneously and seemed to carry more weight than had Asherton's lukewarm agreement.

"I hope so," the personnel director said, rising. As if on cue, the two women who flanked him rose in unison.

"Why don't I call you every Friday morning, just to see if there are minor problems?" Kate volunteered. "The major ones, of course, you can call in immediately. But I'm hoping that soon there won't be any major problems." Her smile was bright and, she hoped, reassuring.

Her idea seemed to please the entourage. This time they volunteered hands, which Kate shook warmly.

She sank back in her seat, watching them file out. Her sigh of relief was audible.

"I'll be right with you," Asherton called after the retreating group. He turned his pale blue eyes on her. "What do you mean by hand carrying the checks to them without clearing it first?" he demanded, dropping the smile he had been sporting for an hour and a half.

"I think it worked very well, Tim," Mike said in a low voice that commanded total respect. He draped his arm across Kate's chair. "Besides, she did clear it. She cleared it with me. I didn't have time to tell you."

"Oh, well." Asherton wavered. "That's different. Good job, Mike. Knew we could count on you." He shook Mike's hand and left without a word to Kate.

She pretended she didn't notice the slight as she meticulously put her papers back into the light tan briefcase.

"I'm sorry he didn't have the decency to acknowledge what you did here," Mike said with genuine sympathy.

Kate shrugged, not looking at him. "Timothy Asherton has spoken through the side of his mouth for so long that I doubt he knows how to give an honest reaction. Besides, he doesn't like me. Actually," she said, looking up, "that's putting it mildly. And the feeling is mutual."

"C'mon," Mike said, his arm about her shoulder, "I'll buy you a well-deserved lunch."

Suddenly Kate felt very happy.

Lunch was delightful. Kate was proud of herself for having saved the account, and Mike didn't mince words in telling her that indeed she had done so. To Kate, so unused to praise from her superiors, his words were like honey to her soul.

"To Kate Lonigan," he said now, raising his wineglass. "May your next triumph include me too." His eyes spoke volumes to her, shining seductively in the light from the candles on their table. The restaurant Mike had chosen was dimly lit, even at noon.

Kate sipped her wine, looking at him over the rim of her glass. Who was this mysterious stranger who had added so much to her life? He was magnetic, dynamic, sensual to the point of distraction, and totally mysterious. But while mystery could serve as an attention getter early on, once a relationship was on its feet, it only got in the way. Mike's secretiveness and his possible motives for it were an ever-present thorn in her side. If she thought about the matter unemotionally she knew that he had to keep his "mission" under wraps. But she couldn't view it unemotionally. She was involved—hopelessly, utterly involved. And she needed some more definite token of his feelings for her. Trust could go a long way in that direction, she mused. But trust was obviously not forthcoming on either side. Kate continued to study him.

"You did a great job today," he repeated. "Should we go out tonight and celebrate?"

She was tempted. But she had rehearsal tonight, and she couldn't afford to miss it. Opening night was looming closer and closer. She shook her head. "I'm afraid not."

"I thought you said you weren't afraid of anything," he said, amused.

She chose her words carefully. "Perhaps I should have said, I'm sorry, but I can't make it."

"So am I," he said softly. He seemed actually to mean it. Which was real? The teasing man with the wicked twinkle in his eye or the man who spoke softly to her? The man who flirted equally with Gay Ling and her or the one who seemed to have eyes only for her? The one who invited intimacy or the one who withdrew his trust the moment she probed? Kate sighed. It didn't matter, did it? No matter what his guise, he still had the power to make her blood rush, to rouse her to unknown peaks.

They finished their meal and left the dim restaurant, their eyes blinking at the unaccustomed brightness of the day.

"How about Sunday?" Mike asked suddenly as they were driving back.

Kate was surprised at the question abruptly breaking the comfortable silence between them. "How about Sunday for what?" she asked.

"Dinner. And perhaps I could also return your car."

There was no rehearsal on Sunday. A broad smile appeared on her face. She nodded. "Sunday's fine," she said. You'll be sorry, a voice echoed inside her.

"Good, I'll call you first," he told her.

She wondered if he had some sort of business to take care of, the way he had had that first weekend they were together.

Sunday came an eternity later, after a grueling rehearsal on Friday night. There were so many problems that Sam Jakes called for another rehearsal the following afternoon. Kate held her breath, praying he wouldn't find it necessary in his temperamental heart to call a rehearsal for Sunday, too. He didn't.

Mike had promised to phone her before making final arrangements for dinner. But Friday night and Saturday went by without a word from him. Kate began to worry.

Where was her cool, she demanded of herself, staring at the bedroom mirror on Sunday morning. What had this man done to her during the short time she'd known him? The telephone rang as she was furiously brushing her hair. Gladys managed to beat her to it.

"It's him!" she called out with all the finesse of a kid sister. Frowning, Kate took the phone from her hand.

She heard Mike's chuckle the moment she put the phone to her ear. "How's my cheering section?" he asked.

"Gladys is fine—for a person who's about to lose her job," Kate said pointedly. Gladys lifted her head indignantly and marched out of earshot.

"Is an hour too soon?" he asked.

"For what?" she asked cautiously.

"To pick you up."

"But it's only ten o'clock. Where are we having dinner? Europe?"

He laughed. "I thought we'd spend the day together."

The prospect brought goose bumps to her flesh. "An hour will do," she replied coolly. "What shoud I wear?" For daytime the rather formal dress she had planned to wear would clearly be inappropriate.

"As little as possible," he told her.

"I'll wear a coat of armor," she replied.

"Just so long as you remember the can opener. See you soon."

Kate went back to her closet and riffled through her clothes. Nothing seemed suitable. She finally chose a green two-piece dress with a form-fitting skirt. The top had a zipper that ran from chin to waist. She zipped it only to the point where her cleavage began. Then she dabbed an expensive perfume behind either ear and on her wrist, and pinned up her hair elaborately. Viewing the results from all angles, she was satisfied: not too dressy, not too casual. No matter what restaurant they went to, she ought to be properly clad.

Kate was just blowing on her freshly polished nails when the doorbell rang. Testing gingerly, she found them to be dry and went to open the door. Gladys had already admitted Mike and was chatting with him like an old friend. Gladys, Kate noted, had that habit, held over from her early days on the nightclub circuit. She always talked to people as if she had known them for years.

"There she is. Got herself pretty well dolled up, for a change," Gladys said, gesturing at Kate as she walked into the room. "The Porsche is back," she added.

Mike's liquid eyes enveloped every inch of her body as he nodded his approval. "The lady is as lovely as she is bright," he said, offering her his arm.

"Oh, Kate," Gladys said, rolling her eyes. "He's divine," she added in a low stage whisper. "Let me tell you, Kate, that's the best—"

"Save it, Gladys," Kate muttered under her breath as she passed the housekeeper on her way to the door.

Mike had the grace to pretend he hadn't heard.

"Thanks for returning my car," Kate told him as she slid her long legs into his Mercedes. "What do I owe you?"

Mike merely shrugged. "It was on the house," he said. "Or on the garage, rather. The chief mechanic insisted. It isn't often he gets to work on a car like yours."

"But—"

"Trust me," Mike said, holding up his hand. He started the engine.

"Well...thanks," said Kate, hesitantly. "Um...where are we going?"

"You'll see," Mike told her, shutting his door.

"Always the mysterious stranger." She watched him from the corner of her eyes as he maneuvered the car out of the driveway.

Mike only chuckled. Kate eased back against the plush leather seat and watched as the desert scenery zipped by.

"Well?" she asked finally.

"Well, what?" Mike countered innocently.

"Where are you taking me?"

"To the ends of the earth, to paradise, to where the west wind meets the eastern sun..." he began grandly, his eyes teasing her as he glanced in her direction.

"You're taking me to your place, aren't you?" she said, sinking into the deep cushion.

"Could be," he said, grinning.

"We shouldn't—"

"Oh, but we should," Mike insisted playfully, reaching for her hand.

"Let me rephrase that. *I* shouldn't," Kate said, even while everything within her cried out, Yes!

"You'll break Marguerite's heart."

"Marguerite?" she echoed. "And just who is Marguerite?"

"She's my cleaning woman. I found out she's a great cook as well. She's been slaving all day making Sunday dinner for us."

"Well, I suppose we can't disappoint Marguerite," Kate said, allowing the faintest touch of a smile.

Mike reached over and squeezed her hand. "Atta girl."

The feel of his hand on hers made her pulse jump. She felt like a schoolgirl thrilling to her first male touch. Kate sighed. She felt so warm and close to this man. To think that only a month before he had been a total stranger.

Suddenly she felt as though she were shot through with sunlight, all from Mike's magic touch.

For a moment she looked at him fondly, noting the outline of the dimple in his cheek. She found herself wanting to reach out and touch it, to trace its curve. The dimple made him look almost boyish. But she had never felt like this around any boy, she reminded herself.

As they entered Mike's minihacienda, she wondered what Marguerite would be like. The house had a lovely Old World charm. Would Marguerite?

Kate had envisioned a fiery, voluptuous, dark-eyed girl with long hair and swaying hips, and a tray—symbol of her servitude to Mike. When Marguerite finally appeared, the tray was the only accurate part of the prediction. On it were cool drinks and sandwiches. Marguerite herself was several inches shorter than Kate and a hundred pounds heavier. Her gray-streaked hair was pulled back into a bun at the nape of her neck, and the swirling, wide skirt and blouse she wore made a windstorm of colors.

Mike laughed softly as he took the tray from his housekeeper's hands and turned toward Kate. "Not what you expected, I take it?" His voice was low. "Thank you. I won't be needing anything right now," he said, nodding his thanks to Marguerite.

"No," she agreed, casting a warm, approving eye over Kate. "You seem to have everything you need."

As she trundled off, a burst of color, Kate shook her head. The resemblance to Gladys was uncanny. She turned back to Mike, who was setting two places at the massive coffee table. The furniture was all sturdy and masculine. Everywhere Kate's eyes went, they met solid dark wood. Even the lamps were wood based. Mike's home had the look of an old-fashioned hacienda. Kate liked it. She wondered at the expense he had gone to for a house that would be only temporary. Or did he have other plans?

Her heart leaped for a moment, but she forced down the thought.

"Marguerite's the greatest," Mike was saying, motioning for Kate to take a seat. "A little impertinent, maybe, but it keeps things interesting. Have a jalapeño sandwich."

"This is the Sunday dinner she's been slaving over?" Kate asked skeptically, raising one well-curved brow as she looked at Mike.

"This is only the first course. Mexican hors d'oeuvres. Besides," he added, trying to look solemn, "it takes precision to make the perfect sandwich." He held up one small square. "Just look at how neatly the corners are cut. That takes time, Kate."

"You're quite a salesman."

"If I sold so well, we wouldn't be sitting here talking," he said significantly.

It was time to change the topic. "I've been trying to figure out what nationality you are," Kate said airily.

"Have you, now?" Mike smiled warmly. He took a sandwich and leaned back. "I'm Welsh, actually," he said. "On my father's side. My mother was a little bit of everything, including Cherokee Indian." He watched her reaction.

"That explains it, then."

"What?"

"The way you stalk a person."

He moved closer. "I don't have a tomahawk in my hand, though."

"I'm not sure that's a relief," she replied, reaching for a tall, frosty glass of sangria. "At least then I'd know your intentions."

"All you have to do is look into my eyes to know my intentions," he told her. And how well she knew the danger of looking into his eyes! "And," he continued, putting down the sandwich as he stroked her back with silky movements, "I'll be glad to show you."

"Marguerite—"

"Rhymes with 'discreet,' and she is."

"I'm sure she's had plenty of practice," Kate countered. But her remark only seemed to amuse him.

"I'd love to see what goes on in your mind. You seem to think of me as a seasoned playboy. I wish it were true. Actually," he said, rising, "I've been too busy to indulge in the sort of life you've planned for me."

"I haven't planned anything for you," Kate retorted. "And you don't seem to need a bit of help," she added as he got up to flip a switch on the far wall beneath the ornate chandelier that hung over the ball-and-claw-foot oak table. Warm vibrations of romantic music filled the air.

"Actually," Mike told her, his eyes a soft caress, "your cooperation would be help enough . . ." He stood before her, his legs slightly apart, creating an image of total sexual maleness. "I don't suppose you dance?" His question surprised her.

"At noon? Seldom."

"Why not?"

"No reason," she conceded.

"Does that mean you will?"

"Oh, why not." Kate rose to face him, her hands ready to be taken in his.

He pressed her close as the music infused their bodies. Kate sighed. The touch of his breath on her neck gave birth to the warmest sensations inside. Her eyes closed almost involuntarily. Suddenly she knew peace.

# CHAPTER
## *Seven*

EVER SO SLOWLY Kate's body relaxed against Mike's as he held her closer still, and the music filled her senses. She loved being enclosed in his strong arms. She loved feeling his body so close to hers. One romantic melody after another floated through the large parquet-floored room, which saw only a little of the afternoon sun. All that was missing, she mused, was a fire in the brick fireplace, but it was much too warm for that. And growing warmer.

She rested her head against his broad chest, aware of its heat beneath her cheek. He was wearing a blue shirt, rolled up at the sleeves and partially open in the front. It made him look even more rugged and devil-may-care than she had thought possible.

As the last song ended, Mike lifted her chin with his crooked finger and kissed her softly. She felt herself melting against him.

"You're trying to seduce me," she said, rousing herself and fighting for her senses.

"How'm I doing?" he asked, kissing one closed eyelid and then another. She thought she'd never felt anything gentler in her life and fought even harder for control.

"Too well," she said and stopped dancing to wander about the room as if she were suddenly intrigued with the decor. The Spanish flavor of the design was brought out quite clearly. It was most evocative.

"You've done a terrific decorating job," Kate said, trying to keep her voice light. Mike appeared behind her, putting his arms about her waist and pulling her close. She felt his breath on her neck a scarce moment before his lips were there, his small kisses causing flames of desire to course through her body.

"Actually, it's not mine." Aha, thought Kate. Temporary, indeed. "The owner's in Europe at the moment," Mike continued. "And I'm in Nevada," he said in a teasing whisper that made him almost irresistible. Kate laughed, lightly, she hoped. In truth, her laugh sounded nervous to her own ears. Was she nervous? Well, if she wasn't, she was a damn fool, her common sense told her.

"I've done something with the bedroom—"

"Worn it out, no doubt."

Mike laughed gently. "Oh, Katie, you're really too much." He turned her around and took hold of her hands. "So, if you don't want to be seduced—yet," he added with the hint of a smile—had he read her mind?—"and you don't want a tour of the house, what would you like to do?"

"I wouldn't mind a little conversation," she said. "There's a lot I don't know about you, Mike."

"Okay," he said, pulling her back to the couch. "Let's talk. I see those questions in your eyes. What is it you want to know about me?"

Suddenly Kate didn't know where to start. She didn't want to sound overly eager.

"All right, I'll make it easy for you," he offered. "My roots are very humble." The bantering tone slowly subsided as he continued.

"My father was a real-estate salesman—an unsuccessful real estate salesman. He couldn't've sold air conditioners in hell. He's retired now," Mike mused. "A real great guy, though. Anyway," he continued, "Dad barely provided the food for the table. Mom was the real provider. She waited tables. In college I had scholarships, and most years I held down two jobs. One of them was a summer internship at Icon. When I graduated, that's where I went.

"My drive to succeed at Icon—all that 'boy wonder' stuff—had a lot to do with my parents. I wanted to buy them a house and make sure they never wanted for anything else in their lives. I have one younger sister who's unspoiled, even though she's a heartbreaker," he said with a fond grin. "She lives with them and goes to the local college. I never had time to be an Eagle Scout, but I did help several old ladies cross the street when I finished my paper route early. Any other questions?" He eyed her low neckline.

"No," said Kate, touched by what he had said but striving to keep her light tone. "But I'd like it if you took your eyes off my chest."

"If you'd unzip that zipper a bit, maybe I'd consider it," he teased, reaching for the pull.

"Please," said Kate frostily. She covered the zipper with her hand.

"Aww." Mike's fingers brushed her face, sending a warm flood of vibrations through her.

Kate rose. "How about showing me around?"

Mike grinned. "Your wish is my command," he said.

They toured the one-story circular house. All the halls

led to a charming central courtyard that housed a fountain surrounded by cherubs with impish grins. He'd probably trained them, Kate thought. They sat down on the marble bench beside the fountain, and Kate watched the cascading water splash lightly from one tier to another, disappearing amid soft bubbles in the bottom basin.

"You're awfully pensive," he told her. "Are you always?"

She shrugged. "There was always so much noise in my house, I learned to be quiet and observe."

"You're a rare woman," Mike said.

"These compliments that trip off your tongue," she said, smiling, determined not to take them to heart. "Do they come easily to you?"

"When the inspiration is right," he said, stopping to look at her. The afternoon sun shone warmly against her head. Suddenly Mike's strong hand was cupping it from behind. One by one he removed the pins, undoing the hairdo she had taken such pains to get right.

"What are you doing?" she protested. Her hands flew up.

"I like it better down," he murmured, putting the pins in his pocket and fanning out her hair. "There, you look like a golden nymph. The other way you looked too unapproachable."

"That might have been the idea," she lied.

"I don't think so," he murmured, bending his head toward hers.

She looked off to the side. "I—I forgot to thank you for lying to Asherton for me and saying that you had okayed my carrying those checks."

Mike followed her lead and began to walk. "It was a good idea. I should have thought of it myself."

Kate's reply was lost in Marguerite's plaintive wail as they reentered the house through the kitchen. Her dark brows were knit in a scowl, and she was muttering angrily in Spanish. On the chocolate-color tile of the sink counter were lined all the elements of a perfect Mexican dinner, but Marguerite glared past them into the sink.

"What's the matter, Marguerite?" Mike asked, closing the door behind him.

"The sink!" She gestured angrily at it. "The water won't go down. Just sit there." She folded her arms across her ample bosom and looked expectantly at her employer.

Mike sighed and rolled up his sleeves even farther. "Okay, Marguerite, hold onto your bustle. Let me get my tools."

Kate followed him into the garage. "I thought you weren't mechanically inclined," she said.

He grinned sheepishly. "I couldn't think of another way to get you into my car that night."

Her eyes grew wide. "Then it *was* you who fixed my car!"

"Guilty," he said, raising his hand solemnly.

*"That's* why there was no bill!"

"Payment can be tendered in another fashion, if you prefer," he said. He seemed about to kiss her, despite the fact that he had a plunger in one hand and a toolbox in the other. But a sudden loud grinding sound caught their attention.

"Hold on, Marguerite," Mike called, stepping back into the house, with Kate following. He placed the tool-box on the kitchen floor and looked down at the black liquid now floating in the sink.

"I thought the disposal might help," Marguerite said in response to his inquiring look.

Mike got to work, and Kate spent the next half-hour watching him, offering tools at his command while he lay flat on his back under the sink. It was such a domestic scene that she couldn't help being tickled by it. Finally he was finished. When he got up from under the sink to try the faucet, she saw that his shirt was soaked through. His efforts were rewarded, though, as they watched the water flow freely down the drain.

Marguerite began to shoo him out of the kitchen so she could finish the dinner preparations. "That's gratitude for you," Mike said as Marguerite gave him a hefty push.

Kate laughed, following him through the courtyard into what turned out to be his bedroom.

"Sure you're not afraid to be here?" he teased. She stood leaning against the doorway. "I mean, the way you've avoided my best moves lately . . ."

"I'm getting better," she said, eyeing his large brass bed with its deep brown comforter.

"Don't get too good," he said, poking his head out of his closet as he went in search of another shirt. "You won't have any fun."

"Perhaps." Her eyes glided over Mike's muscular, smooth chest as he stripped off his shirt and put on a fresh one. His muscles rippled with every movement. It unsettled her just to watch him. She was sure he was taking his time at it, just to make her uncomfortable. Then he slipped his hands about her waist.

"I guess dinner's in order shortly—unless you'd like to stop for a second appetizer. We have time."

Despite her slightly weakened knees, Kate turned and headed back through the courtyard toward the dining room, taking a shortcut. All the rooms could be reached in two fashions, either through the house or through the courtyard, which was a more direct path.

Mike followed silently and went to the bar along the back wall to mix a cocktail. "Have I told you how irresistible you look today?" he asked.

"Not in so many words," Kate replied flippantly, sitting down on the other side of the bar. "But I think I get the picture." Smiling, she accepted the margarita he handed her.

"Then why won't you hold still?" Mike asked as he came around to join her.

"Because I'm not sure I trust you," she said bluntly.

He laughed, shaking his head. "Okay, let's stay on neutral ground for a while. How do you think the office is running?" he asked. "Are my changes working?"

To look at him now Kate could almost believe that this was his only concern—a smoothly functioning office. If she hadn't picked up on that phone call, she wouldn't have suspected anything else.

"Look at your weekly count," she replied. "The numbers connected with production are going up while errors are going down. What more proof do you need? That, and the circle of fans that gape at your closed door every day should tell you everything you need to know." She flicked her tongue lightly across the rim of the glass, savoring the salt.

"Not everything," Mike said. He looked at her pointedly. "It still doesn't tell me everything about you."

"I thought I was in the clear," she said dryly. "Or is your investigation on again?"

"I'm speaking in my personal capacity, not my professional one. Forget I'm office manager. I want to know about *you.*"

"Okay. What is it you want to know? I thought you had covered all the points before." She caught the last few grains of salt with her tongue and set the glass down.

"I want to know everything," he said. "Right down to the color of your underwear."

"Please," she said, trying to mask her growing embarrassment. See, she told herself. He wasn't serious about her, he was serious about getting her into bed. In the next moment she was wondering why she cared. Her own gaze swam under the force of his intent green eyes. How long could a woman hold out? If this be folly, she thought suddenly, let's make the most of it.

She leaned forward slightly.

It was all the encouragement Mike needed. He leaned, too, and soon his mouth was on hers, soft and probing.

His tongue found hers, and Kate's breath quickened. It was that moment Marguerite chose to enter, bearing dinner.

"Go on," she urged as they pulled hastily apart. "I see nothing. I am only bringing your dinner. See, already I am gone," and with that the door shut firmly behind her.

"You really do have her trained well." Kate laughed, sliding off the bar stool.

"Best money can buy," Mike said, crossing over to the window and closing the blinds so that very little light came in. He came to the round table and lit the two tall perfumed candles that were balanced in silver holders.

"Do you have a gypsy violinist in your pocket?" Kate asked as he pushed in her chair for her.

"No, I want to be alone with you," he said, his voice husky.

Dinner was delicious. Kate ate slowly, the romantic mood permeating every pore of her being. Mike, for his part, did try to keep a light conversation going. Kate struggled with her emotions.

What exquisite torture, though, she mused as she finished Marguerite's superb chocolate mousse.

"Can I get you anything else?" Mike asked as she pushed back her plate.

"Possibly a crane to get me out of this chair," she said. "I feel so fat."

"Every ounce is beautifully packed," he assured her. "And I don't suppose you weigh more than a hundred pounds dripping wet, with seaweed draped all around you." He pulled back her chair and led her to the living room.

The sound of her heels on the hard bare floor was all that interrupted the steady beat of the music that still played, pulsing around them like a misty veil.

"Some wine?" he asked, nodding toward the bar.

She shook her head no, then changed her mind. "Well,

maybe a little," she said, holding up her thumb and forefinger to show him how much.

Mike brought back a full glass. "You're tense," he justified. "Here, turn around." He sat down behind her.

"I'm not tense," she insisted but did as he bid her. His strong fingers began to knead the knots in her shoulders and neck, causing a delicious, soothing feeling to pass through her. His fingers continued weaving their magic, moving down her spine, and she had no idea when they managed to slip under her blouse and work their way to the front after having unhooked her bra and ever so gently slipped the gauzelike material away from her breasts.

Her emotions burst into flame in the center of her being as his hands covered her breasts. Languidly he teased and stroked until she thought she would scream. Then, ever so slowly, he turned her to face him, taking possession of her mouth, stopping any words of protest that might have formed on her lips. The kiss grew and grew, sapping her strength and all her common sense, replacing it with a fiery desire that ate into her very soul. His tongue searched out the contours of her mouth, exciting her even further before his lips left her, kissing the sensitive hollow of her throat, his lips following the path made by her zipper. Soon it was completely open. He lifted his head slightly to gaze at her, and she knew that she should stop him, that she should protect her breasts from his burning eyes, but she was totally powerless to do so. His raging desire thrilled her, matching her own as he lowered his head once more, covering first one nipple and then another with his warm lips, circling them with his tongue until she arched her back, wanting to be even closer, wanting more, more . . .

He pushed her back against the sofa, deep into the tan cushions. The length of his long body met hers. Kate was aware of every hard contour. She wanted to be even more aware, wanted to feel him deep inside her. She was drowning in the waves of passion he had stirred; she couldn't find a lifeline.

"Oh, Kate, Kate," he murmured huskily against her hair. "Come to me."

Yes, yes, her body told him. Oh, Mike, yes. From far away came the chime of a doorbell. Kate's eyes flew open. Marguerite might be discreet, but now here was someone else.

Her senses came crashing in around her as the identity of the caller, whose voice could be heard clearly from the nearby hall, became apparent. It was Gay Ling.

Kate gasped, trying to regain control of her emotions. Quickly she arranged her clothes, zipping up the top. There was only time to run her fingers briefly through her hair before the commotion outside became a shrill crescendo.

"But he *is* home," she heard Gay's lilting voice insist. "His car is in the garage. It's quite important, really—"

"No, not at home, not at home," Marguerite's Spanish-inflected voice repeated firmly.

"I insist..." There was the sound of a loud scuffle. Mike jumped up and strode to the door. He opened it. Marguerite was literally dragging the fragile Eurasian woman away. In terms of sheer size Gay was no match for Marguerite.

Mike scowled. "That's enough, Marguerite," he said, though it was clear his annoyance was directed at Gay. "What do you want?" he asked.

Gay shuddered, brushing off the shoulder of her sheer silk blouse and glaring at Marguerite, who still hovered nearby. Then she saw Kate. Her eyes widened in surprise.

"I—I'm sorry," she murmured. "I had no idea—"

Kate looked directly at her. "Of what, Gay?"

"I...my earrings." The woman stumbled over her words. "I left my jade earrings...here. Last night."

Kate's mouth dropped open. So, he *was* playing them off against each other! Gay Ling had been here just last night! "Where's the phone?" Kate demanded of Marguerite. "I'd like to call a cab."

"I—I didn't mean to interrupt anything," Gay said. Kate caught just a glimmer of mischief in her tip-tilted eyes. Well, she couldn't care less. Gay was welcome to him. All Kate wanted was out.

"What could you possibly have interrupted?" she snapped acidly. She turned to glare at Mike. "Mike was outlining his new office policies for me, just as I'm sure he was doing with you. Last night."

And with that she stalked out to the kitchen behind a reluctant Marguerite. Mike, who had stood with his arms crossed as the little scene unfolded, did nothing to stop her. "You're making a big mistake," said the plump Mexican woman.

Kate grabbed the receiver. "My mistake was coming here," she said.

But the housekeeper shook her head. "He cares for you," she said. "He does not care for that other one. And if he did, you would still be making a mistake. A good man is worth fighting for. Did you never learn that?"

Kate regarded her angrily. She waited for Marguerite to explain Gay's presence here last night, waited for Mike to come after her and explain it himself. Neither event took place. Marguerite resumed loading the dishwasher, a task that had apparently been interrupted by Gay's appearance. "A big mistake," the woman muttered, carefully placing a glass. "Are you afraid to fight?"

"I won't fight for a man," Kate said, looking directly into Marguerite's accusing eyes as she dialed Information.

"Why not?" the older woman demanded. *"She* does." She gave a quick nod toward the other room.

"Well, I don't," said Kate firmly.

"Hello?" the voice in the receiver was saying. Kate

watched as Marguerite shrugged in annoyance and left the room, mumbling something in Spanish.

Mechanically Kate asked for the number of Kwick Cab, the local service. The sound of Gay Ling's laughter rang in her ears. Kate gripped the receiver tighter. If she had jumped to the wrong conclusion, where was Mike to explain otherwise? Busy entertaining Gay. She and Gay were probably interchangeable to him. Perhaps he even preferred Gay; many a man had. "Hello?" she said.

Moments later Kate shut the front door softly behind herself and made her way to the beckoning light of the cab. No one tried to stop her.

"What happened?" Gladys asked the moment Kate came through the door. "You look like you lost your best friend." She clucked sympathetically, taking Kate's bag from her shoulder and picking up the shoes she had stepped out of. "Didn't he try anything?"

"Yes, he tried something," Kate said, sighing as she sank onto the sofa, curling her feet under her. Her heart was heavy.

"And?"

"Gay—my 'friend' from work—arrived—to look for an earring she thought she lost."

"And you left them together?" Gladys asked incredulously.

Kate held up her hand. "Don't start, Gladys. I have a headache." She held her throbbing temples.

"Well, maybe this will help your headache," the woman said, opening the door to the den.

Kate's mouth dropped open as Keith Logan, the heart-throb of millions, walked into the room grinning.

"Hi, Sis," he said.

# CHAPTER
# *Eight*

KATE JUMPED OFF the sofa and returned her brother's big bear hug. "What are you doing here?" she asked.

"I've got some time off between pictures and I came to see you knock 'em dead in *Rain*. You didn't think I'd miss your debut, did you?" His eyes gleamed merrily.

Kate shot Gladys an accusing look. "How did you know?" she asked him.

"Can't keep things from a twin. You know that, Katie." He loosened his necktie and sat down on the couch. "So, tell me all about yourself. That exchange I just heard between you and Gladys—does that mean you've finally got a guy in your life? Who is he? And is he good enough for you?" he asked, grinning.

Kate regarded her twin brother, who stood a good ten inches taller than she. They didn't look much like twins. His hair was a shade darker, a dirty-blond mop that fell endearingly into his bright blue eyes. His slightly crooked smile was engaging, and Kate thought fondly that she could see exactly what it was about her extroverted brother that made women's hearts flutter.

She hadn't meant to, but there was always something about the affable Keith that made her want to confide in him. It wasn't long before he had probed and prodded from her the entire story of Mike Fleming's arrival at Icon and her—could she call it involvement?—with him. His involvement with both her and Gay Ling, she amended. Keith clucked sympathetically over her description of Gay. "I'd like to meet this siren myself," he said, grinning.

"No, you wouldn't," Kate retorted, throwing a cushion at him.

"I wouldn't, I wouldn't," said Keith, hands to his face in mock terror.

Somehow in the telling Kate felt better. Gladys had outfitted one of the extra bedrooms for Keith. As soon as Kate had seen him to it, she went upstairs to bed. Sleep came immediately. Only her dreams were troubled.

Monday morning's first light came all too swiftly. Keith was still sleeping soundly as Kate prepared for work. As well as by their looks, they were also differentiated by their sleeping habits. Keith liked to sleep late, while Kate liked to see the sunrise and fill the early morning with work. After donning a lavender suit whose jacket cinched in to flatter her narrow waist, and getting a cup of Gladys's coffee, Kate left for the office, making sure she had her script with her. Tonight was one of two final rehearsals before Thursday night's opening performance.

Kate entered the office at seven and found almost a third of the crew already there. Formerly the first shift hadn't been so prompt. There had been a definite change in office atmosphere and, while she couldn't say everyone was eager to work, she heard far fewer complaints.

Yes, Mike had certainly made a difference in their lives—especially in Gay's and hers.

He was late that morning: it was nearly nine before he arrived. Kate had been awaiting him anxiously. She wasn't sure how she'd react. She needn't have worried, however. With him was a large, hulking man who had an air of authority. Clearly this was not a time for personal exchanges. Kate wondered if the man was also from the home office in New York. Maybe he had something to do with the "investigation."

Her curiosity was satisfied within the hour, when Mike buzzed for her to come to his office. He was all business. Not a hint of what had happened the night before could be read on his face as she walked through the door. "Kate," he said, rising, "I'd like you to meet Mr. Gerald Weston, the head of Weston Petroleum and, hopefully, our newest client." The familiar, easy smile spread across his face.

The heavyset man made an attempt to rise, too, then obviously thought better of it when the seat didn't seem willing to relinquish its hold on his ample girth. Weston shifted his cigar to his left hand and shook Kate's outstretched one.

"This is Kate Lonigan," Mike continued, "one of our three second assistant managers. She'll be showing you how our computers will be used to process your claims." Mike turned to Kate. "That all right with you?"

She smiled, liking the confidence he showed in her ability, even if she didn't like him right now. "Fine," she responded.

"All right, shall we?" Mike asked, nodding toward the door of his office.

Kate led the way back to her desk, where she showed Weston the ease with which a claim could now be processed, provided that all the information had been submitted. The little green lights from the screen left the man scratching his head, bemused, as he walked back with Mike to his office, but he seemed impressed—enough so that the following day he called to say that he and his board had voted to go with Icon on a trial basis.

A trial basis, Kate thought to herself. All policies were that. At any moment any of the client companies, if they were dissatisfied, could pull their business without any penalty whatsoever. She supposed this meant they'd landed the Weston account. Her face flushed with pleasure as she digested the news. She knew she was at least partly responsible.

Much to her surprise and chagrin, the Weston account went to Gay's unit. Kate, who had promised herself she wouldn't seek him out, entered Mike's office, the memo announcing the new assignment in hand. "Why?" she asked, setting it on his desk. Maybe she was wrong to care. But she did.

Mike glanced at the memo. His neatly arranged desk held more stacks of paper than it had in the five years Albert Baines had had his position. He seemed to understand immediately. His businesslike demeanor remained, but his eyes were warm and sympathetic. "Because," he said, "although you appear to be a workaholic, I don't want you worked to death. If I spread you too thin, you'll be no good to me at all."

Kate glared at him, a question—*the* question that in one version or another had been on her mind for days—tickling her tongue. "It—it doesn't have anything to do with Sunday, does it?"

There. She had done it. Mike's green eyes narrowed. "Are you implying that I run my office from my bedroom?"

"I'm wondering what you *do* in that bedroom—and with how many women. I'm wondering how you can be with Gay Ling one night and me the next. I—" Kate bit her lip, a little shocked at herself. This was the office! Deeply embarrassed, she looked away, focusing on the scenery outside Mike's window many stories below.

"Kate," he said, rising to take her shoulders. "Please trust me for now. And let me say just one thing. What I feel for you—or anyone else—has nothing to do with what happens here in the office. Do I make myself clear?" he added gently.

Not really, she thought.

"Have dinner with me tonight," he said softly. His long black lashes swept upward, making him look almost unbearably attractive.

"I can't," she muttered. It was true. Tonight was rehearsal, tomorrow dress rehearsal.

"Tomorrow?" he asked evenly.

She shook her head. "I've got—another commitment." She knew she should explain. And yet, why? Why blow her cover? Why increase her self-consciousness on opening night? It was bad enough that Keith would be there. She didn't want her boss there too when she fell flat on her face. And why reveal her secrets, anyway? Mike, after all, had secrets, plenty of them. "Trust me," he had said. What was that supposed to imply?

But already he was nodding, his expression unchanged. Clearly he was undaunted by her refusal—which irked her all the more! He could at least have probed a little. Now he'd probably just ask Gay. Kate gritted her teeth. "Well, okay then," she said and, picking up the memo, went back to her desk.

Mike was gone for the next two days, off on some company business. Control of the office went to Dave, and Kate overheard him telling Milt that it wouldn't be long now before Dave would be in permanent control, since Mike was bound to leave soon.

The thought filled Kate with an abysmal loneliness she tried hard to shut away as she dressed for the opening performance.

She put on a blue-gray jersey that hugged her waist and tied a blue scarf over her hair, keeping it loose. She had set her hair to make it appear fuller and curlier than usual, trying for the windblown effect that she felt Sadie Thompson should have. On the hanger hung Sadie's cheap white dress and large picture hat with its faded feathers.

Keith came over to her as she was about to leave.

"You look terrific," he pronounced.

"I only hope I sound terrific."

"Is there any doubt?" he asked. "After all, you're a Logan—or a Lonigan, take your pick." He laughed. "Besides, you're my twin sister. How can you miss?"

She checked her watch. It was time to leave. "Are you sure you want to come?" Her hand hesitated on the doorknob.

"Wouldn't miss it for the world," he assured her.

"I don't know. It might be boring for you. And if you're recognized, you might get mobbed."

"What do you mean, if?" He laughed again. "That's part of the fun of being me—all those lovely young ladies wanting to be next to me. Ah, it's a wonderful life," he told her with a sigh. "Now hurry or you'll be late. I've got my tickets."

"Tickets?" she asked. "Whom are you bringing?"

"Why, the lady who made this all possible," he told her with a wink. "Gladys," he said as the woman came out, wiping her hands on her apron. He grabbed her by the waist and nuzzled her. "You know I've always had a fondness for older women."

"Go on with you before I take you at your word and teach you a few things," Gladys snapped, but her eyes were bright with pleasure.

"I think I'll leave. Even Sadie Thompson would blush," Kate said, slinging her plastic-encased costume over her shoulder and hurrying out to her car.

\* \* \*

The theater buzzed with nervous, excited voices. Sam was everywhere, the anxiety-ridden director fussing and prompting and generally getting on people's nerves. Everyone was involved in his or her role, but the ones who seemed to be having the most fun were those who played the natives of Pago-Pago, staging a semierotic dance with Sadie as the central figure. This was the scene Reverend Davidson interrupted to deliver his tirade against sin.

Five minutes before the curtain was to go up, one of the actresses ran breathlessly into their communal dressing room backstage to announce that someone had seen Keith Logan in the front row.

"What do you think he's doing here?" one of the young women asked, suddenly displaying a terrible case of nerves.

"Maybe he's looking for local talent. They do that, you know," another said solemnly, unconsciously patting her hair into place as they filed out of the dressing room.

Kate only smiled. She didn't want to spoil their excitement or push herself into the limelight by explaining that Keith was here to see her.

"He's probably looking for a good director," said Sam, who had approached the group in his frantic effort to herd everyone into place. "His brother's style leaves a lot to be desired and his father's had his heyday," he added pompously. The director looked about, clapping his hands. "Places, people, places," he ordered.

Outside, the house lights were dimming. The orchestra, comprised of people in the little theater group who had less trouble making an instrument sing than delivering a line, played a theme that the director had taken from the movie version with Rita Hayworth. A hush fell over the audience.

The curtain went up. After the initial encouraging applause had died down, the opening lines were delivered. To her great surprise Kate found she loved every minute onstage. For an hour and a half she was transformed into a devil-may-care creature who reeked of sexuality and made no excuses to anyone. Her role—that of a prostitute trapped on the island of Pago-Pago in a house full of religious, self-righteous people—was like a breath of fresh air to her. She pulled out all the feelings that she kept locked away inside and called on fiery emotions that even she wasn't aware of. As she abandoned herself to the suggestive dance she performed with the natives and bawdy sailors, she drew on her memory of the sensations she had experienced in Mike's arms.

But she couldn't dwell on thoughts of him for long. The part was too demanding. Sadie was to go through a so-called cleansing, for the director had chosen to stick very closely to the original short story. Kate had to age visibly before her audience. Repentance had taken a toll on her, reducing her temporarily to a mournful, spiritless woman who sat in her rocking chair, staring bleakly out at the rain, her body wrapped in a thin dressing gown with cheap feathers clinging listlessly to it.

When the reverend attempted to seduce her during a prayer session, Kate made sure that even those in the back rows could see the fiery indignation that rose to Sadie's eyes. She pulled herself up to her full height, throwing off the heavy weight of "repentance." Her shrill denunciation of him caused the reverend to cring in remorse.

By the last scene Kate was back in Sadie's gaudy white dress with its strings of pearls and feathers. The look on her face was once more that of haughty triumph. Sadie Thompson had exposed hypocrisy masquerading as goodness.

The applause was thunderous, and Kate beamed, exultant. A bouquet of her favorite pink and white carnations was thrust into her hands by the stage manager, and she smiled in the direction of her brother. But as she prepared to walk off, another bouquet, this one of pink roses, was delivered. She looked at the flowers, puzzled. A questioning glance at Keith brought only a shrug in return. Kate gathered up her flowers and made her way backstage to the communal dressing room.

The room bubbled with happy voices and the heady air of triumph.

"Great job, Kate!" One of the native girls hugged her.

"You weren't so bad yourself." Kate laughed, tugging at the woman's black wig. She felt elated by the applause. Yes, there was something to this grease-paint business, even though theater life was unsettling as a whole. She had been part of it too long not to know all the heartache that went with the territory. But the sound of approval rendered so wholeheartedly could almost make it worthwhile. Kate, still floating at least three inches above-ground, sat down to take off her heavy stage makeup. After so much preshow anxiety, she was almost sorry it was over. Oh well, she consoled herself. Six more shows were scheduled over the next few weeks before *Rain* closed.

A loud knock on the door, accompanied by, "Are you decent?" brought a flutter of voices within.

"Is that . . .?" one actress began.

Kate nodded. "It is," she said, enjoying the adulation her brother received. She was really quite proud of him. She was proud of all her brothers.

"Well, open it!" someone ordered, quickly throwing on a robe.

Kate flung open the door and was engulfed in a bear hug while the other women looked on enviously. "Knew you had it in you!" Keith said, full of enthusiasm as he picked her up and twirled her around like a doll. Her slighter willowy frame made this easy for her robust twin. When they were children, she had always said she was cheated by nature. Now she didn't mind.

"Not bad, kid, not bad," Gladys said, patting her hand

and beaming at her. She was dressed in a vivid green dress that caught the eye right away.

"Thank you for the flowers," Kate said to Keith, sitting down. "Both bouquets."

"I only sent one," he told her. "Carnations—your favorite."

Kate looked at Gladys, who held up her hands. "Don't look at me. I don't earn enough to send flowers, much less roses."

The answer confused Kate even more, but she had no time to ponder as the five other women in the room crowded about her, wanting an introduction to Keith Logan. Kate referred to him as a childhood friend.

"What a childhood!" was one reply.

Kate smiled. If only they knew!

She finished her last introduction, Keith responding in his usual charming manner. Then her brother slipped his arm about her waist. "How long will it take you to dress? I'm taking you out to dinner to celebrate."

Kate was about to answer when she turned around and saw Mike Fleming standing in the doorway.

CHAPTER

*Nine*

MIKE LOOKED LIKE a man who had just had a profound and bitter shock.

Kate stared at him. This was the last place she'd expected to see him. "What—what are you doing here?" she stammered.

"Congratulating you," he said quietly. "For a fine performance."

Keith and Gladys turned to look at him. The other actresses were beginning to murmur jealously under their breaths. "Two of them!" Kate heard. "One better-looking than the next!"

"How did you know I was here?" Kate asked, her head spinning.

"I called you earlier and got Gladys," he said, nodding toward the housekeeper. "She told me where you'd be." His eyes swept over Keith, who smiled genially. "Now I see why you were always so busy. It would have been best to level with me about your friend here." Mike turned to go. "I hope you liked the roses."

Kate grabbed his arm. "Where are you going?" she asked. Her robe gaped open as she strained to hold him.

Mike stopped, gazing down at her body. Kate flushed, realizing her breasts were straining against the white silk slip that had been part of her costume. Quickly she clutched her robe about her, but not before she caught Mike's expression. It told her he wanted to sweep her into his arms and crush her against him. But the look faded.

"You seem to be busy. I thought I'd go home and drink a toast to womanhood," he said, a trace of bitterness in his voice.

Kate put her hands on her hips. "Well, before you go and down any toasts, I think you should drink one to men who don't wait before they jump to conclusions."

All about them people were leaving the theater in street clothes or partial costume, but Kate took no notice.

"I'm not jumping to conclusions," he said. "I just see now why you couldn't be with me all those evenings. You were too busy with Keith Logan."

"And you, of course, live the life of a celibate monk!" she spat, while her mind reeled crazily. What was she saying? They were arguing over a situation that didn't even exist. Was he really jealous?

"Don't you think you'd better go back? You wouldn't want to keep Keith Logan waiting. Judging from the response in there, you'd better grab him now if you want him." Mike turned to go.

"My brother can take care of himself," Kate said softly as she tied her sash. Mike, his back to her, hesitated. "He's the one who taught me karate."

Mike swung slowly around. "Your brother?" he repeated, stunned.

Kate grinned. "My twin."

Mike cocked his head, returning to her side. "You don't look alike at all."

She shrugged. "Fraternal twins don't, generally."

He took her hands in his. "I feel like a fool," he admitted.

Kate took hold of his arm, not wishing to dwell on it. "The roses are beautiful," she said.

"Not half as beautiful as you." He tilted her head toward him. The dim light backstage shone on his eyes as Kate saw the surge of desire there.

"You know, you're right—maybe I had better save my brother. C'mon," she said, taking Mike by the hand and leading the way back to the dressing room.

Keith was having a great time, sitting on the tabletop that had served as Kate's vanity and signing autographs for hordes of well-wishers.

"Dinner might take awhile," Kate whispered as Gladys inched toward them.

"Happy as a clam," Gladys said, nodding at Keith surrounded by pushing women.

"Gladys, I'll never trust you again," Kate said suddenly, trying to look annoyed.

"Why?" she asked hoarsely. "Are you disappointed to see either one? I sent for her brother," she confided to Mike.

Kate chose not to answer. Instead she grabbed her dress from the back of a chair. "I'll be with you in a few minutes," she said.

Dinner lasted until midnight. At that time Keith, pleading fatigue, rose from the dimly lit table. "Time to take Gladys home," he quipped.

"Actually, we're going dancing." Gladys winked, rising. Keith took her hand. "Bet I can dance the pants off him," she added.

"Bet she can, too," Keith shot over his shoulder. Kate

watched her brother escort the feisty, lovable little woman through the double doors of Carson City's finest restaurant. Her eyes misted for a moment.

"Any other brothers you'd like to tell me about?" Mike asked, searching her face in the flickering light.

"Don't you know about the rest of the family?" Kate asked, taking a sip of her wine. "I guess I'd better warn you. My father is Sean Logan."

"The director?" Mike asked in surprise.

She nodded. "Dad was and still is a perfectionist. He always expected the best—and got it. Brian became a producer; Patrick followed in Dad's footsteps and became a director; and Keith, the best-looking of the bunch, became an actor."

Mike nodded as though he was searching his memory. Clearly he wasn't a movie buff. Most fans knew the family history by heart. His eyes swept her form as he digested this new information. "And what about you?" he asked finally. "You don't want to disappoint Daddy, either, do you?"

Kate shrugged.

"You, too, seem to have bitten by the theater bug," he prodded.

"I enjoy it," she admitted. "It's comforting to immerse yourself in someone else's personality. That way you can express things you'd never have dared to in your own life. Then," she continued thoughtfully, "it's all over when the curtain's down. You're you again."

"And Icon?"

"Icon's my life, for now. And acting is a my hobby."

"So you won't be running back to Hollywood?"

She shook her head. Not so long as you're here, was the silent part of her reply.

They locked glances for a long moment.

"Is it my imagination, or are you relieved?" Kate asked.

"Possibly." He grinned. "What brought you to Icon in the first place?"

"I wanted to pull my life together by myself. I wanted to prove I could make it without being someone's daughter or sister. I love my family dearly," she added, her chin pointing proudly and a smile tugging at her lips, "don't get me wrong. But there's a stigma attached to being Sean Logan's little girl. I wanted to make it as an *ordinary* person, as an insurance exec."

"You're pretty special, though, all on your own, without the Hollywood background." Mike took her hand. Kate felt the warm pressure of his fingers locking about hers. Right now he made her feel special. Very special.

She smiled and leaned forward. Looking into his eyes, she found that she enjoyed being lost in their mesmerizing power.

"Tell me more," she murmured, striving for a light tone. But Mike had woven his spell again.

"I'd rather show you," he whispered huskily.

"Here?"

"Anywhere," he replied. For a fleeting moment he looked somber. Then his smile was back. "Care to dance?" he asked, nodding toward the dance floor, which was illuminated by swirling lights from the multisurfaced silver ball overhead. The music was soft and low.

"Yes, I think I'd like that," Kate murmured, allowing him to lead her to the floor.

She molded her body against his as he held her fast. Barely moving, they swayed to the strains of the ballad. Kate rested her head against his broad shoulder, thrilling to the feel of his heartbeat against hers. Aware of every inch of his body, suddenly she ached to be as free as Sadie Thompson had been.

Someone tapped her on the shoulder. Kate looked up to see one of the other actresses.

"Listen, Kate, I don't care which one it is, but can I

have the one you don't want?" she whispered, looking with appreciative eyes at Mike. "What's your secret, anyway?"

"Clean living, Alice, clean living," Kate murmured. Shaking her head, the girl departed.

# CHAPTER
## *Ten*

HER HEAD RESTING against the plush leather seat of Mike's car, Kate closed her eyes. The excitement of the evening was wearing off, and she was tired. Her head dropped to Mike's shoulder, and he slung an arm around her. Presently Kate opened her eyes.

"Where are we going?" she asked, puzzled. She had assumed Mike would head for the theater, where she'd left her car. She watched his profile, etching it onto her heart as the street lamps they passed outlined it dramatically.

"My place." Mike braked for a stop sign. "I've got some champagne sitting on ice in anticipation of celebrating your triumph." His eyes twinkled.

Kate ignored the warning flash her mind was sending. "What's the harm in a drink?" she heard herself murmur.

She found out less than twenty minutes later. Sitting before a fire in the massive fireplace in Mike's living room, she learned that her defenses were being quickly stripped away with each sip of champagne. Oh, her common sense was still there, urging her not to leave herself so open, to go now before she tasted forbidden fruit that would hold her forever captive. But that voice was getting tinier and more removed by the moment. Still, it struggled valiantly. Kate ignored it.

Mike put his drink down on the coffee table before them, his eyes obviously busy with the planes of her face that were highlighted, like his, by the fire.

"I'd—I'd better be leaving," Kate said in hushed tones, although she made no move to rise. She felt as if she were melting against the heat of his slow-moving fingers that brushed against her cheek ever so softly.

"Shhh," Mike whispered, his breath grazing her face in warm, sensuous waves.

"Please don't," she said hoarsely.

Mike's lips touched the hollow of her throat. "You said you were interested in office morale," he reminded her, taking the drink from her trembling fingers as he slipped his arms about her waist.

"I—am . . ." she breathed.

"Well, I'm part of the office," he said, punctuating each word with light, feathery kisses to her face, her eyes, her brow. "How about my morale?"

"Is this how you usually get your way?" she managed to ask, sinking quickly.

"There's nothing usual about this," he promised her, slipping some of the pins out of her hair and fanning out the tumbling mass of silvery ringlets.

"Mike, no . . ." But there was no conviction in her voice.

Mike took her face in his hands, raising her mouth to his as his lips devoured the hungry sweetness offered.

She was only dimly aware of the fact that as he kissed her, Mike's fingers were loosening the top of her dress. As the dress slipped from her shoulders, leaving her naked on top but for the laciest of pale blue bras, Kate felt a corresponding warmth take hold of the rest of her body. She was supposed to be keeping him at bay, she thought helplessly. But she wanted this man, whatever the consequences that lay hidden ahead. She had never wanted to be held and made love to so badly in her life.

"I don't think we should be doing this," she murmured against his mouth as it assaulted her lips, claiming her life and breath for its own.

"You're outranked," Mike told her huskily, his voice not quite so teasing as it had been. Deftly he unhooked the single catch of her bra, languidly sliding the material away, tugging at it slowly so that the very motion of it moving away from her breasts excited her. His dark head traveled from her lips down to the hollow of her throat, urgent yet maddeningly thorough. Kate arched her breasts against him, wanting to feel his skin, wanting to feel his mouth burning against her.

Some instinct quite apart from common sense caused her to reach up and tug at his pullover shirt, to remove the barrier between them. The shirt adhered well to his muscular frame, making it difficult to remove. Then she felt the heat of his body pressing against her. The soft fabric of the shirt both tickled her and excited her, causing her nipples to harden demandingly as she swayed against him.

His hands and his mouth were everywhere, encasing her in warm velvet, a feeling that grew and grew, making her ache for fulfillment.

"Take your shirt off," she murmured with effort, and he stripped it off in a pantherlike motion. His muscles rippled. Kate couldn't take her eyes from him, or from the seductive smile on his lips. He pushed her down on the sofa, then loomed over her. He paused that way for a long moment.

"This is a hell of a time to be taking inventory," she heard herself say as his hands covered first one breast and then another, stroking lovingly.

"Inventory is the best part," he told her, taking the elastic waist of her skirt and tugging at it so that it slid down first to her hips, then farther and farther, while his lips kissed a path on the growing expanse of exposed skin.

The yearning in her mounted to a heightened crescendo as the heat of the moment increased. There was no turning back now, or any desire to. His strong, sure hands explored her body as if it were a finely tuned instrument; it sang to his strokes. Mike Fleming brought forth responses that Ryan Kilpatrick had not begun to evoke.

Her head swimming, Kate sought to allow words to form on her tongue. But he had rendered her breathless and nearly senseless in a few short master strokes, pitching her into timelessness.

"Where are you taking me?" she heard a faraway voice ask him just as she felt herself scooped into brawny arms. It was as if she had no weight at all. It was like the climactic moment in *Gone With The Wind,* which, as a child, she had watched over and over in her father's private screening room. But never in her wildest dreams had she experienced it. Not like now.

"To my bedroom," he whispered.

She clung to him, feeling the exciting, comforting warmth of his chest against hers as he carried her to his darkened room. Ever so gently he set her down on the bed. All she could see was his face, a mixture of teasing promise and impassioned desire. She wanted to reach up and pull him toward her. As though he were reading her thoughts, Mike dropped down at her side, enfolding her in his arms, stroking her over and over. She moaned without control, tiny gasps of pleasure and desire.

His assault came on two fronts. His lips drank her sweetness, leaving flames in their wake, while his hands caressed her to the point of almost total frenzy. She had never wanted anything or anyone so desperately in her life as she wanted him.

Quaking against the velvet brown bedspread, Kate was just barely aware of the fact that his hands were on either side of her hips, rhythmically slipping her lace panties away, replacing her last shred of clothing with his hot gaze, which devoured every inch of her and made her feel like the most desirable woman in the world. She saw herself mirrored in his liquid green eyes. She had been right in her earlier fantasies. Everything about him smoldered of sexual prowess.

She had no idea when and how the rest of his clothing had been shed. She only knew the infinite excitement of his lean, powerful body descending on hers, moving to become one with hers, his every rippling motion finding expression in her own answering pulse.

Kate moaned softly. She had no identity, no name, nothing but the beating desire to be one with this man. The fierceness of her emotion surprised her. It was something quite foreign to her, something new, something wonderful, something to be remembered and cherished. But not now. Now there was only the desire for fulfillment. She could feel the hard imprint of his body pressing against hers with growing urgency until she thought she couldn't stand it another second. Reaching up, she grasped his shoulders, pulling him down toward her, arching her body up to meet his. She wanted him to feel the same madness that had seized her.

One hand slipped beneath her buttocks, caressing them, pressing them up against him, and then he parted her legs with his own, beginning the final wave to rapture. Dimly Kate was aware of his hypnotic eyes swimming above her, looking at her almost strangely. It was as if perhaps — just perhaps — his response was as new to him as hers was to her.

But then the last tiny thought ebbed, and Kate was

engulfed in being loved by Mike. She felt as if she were being taken to a cliff so high that there was no earthly way to scale it. Vaguely she heard herself gasp for breath as heaven and paradise came to claim her. For one solitary island of time she wanted nothing more in life than to be his forever.

She hadn't realized that her eyes were squeezed shut until she opened them. Mike was next to her, holding her in his arms. There was nothing but silence, save for the rhythmic sound of his breathing and the pounding of her heart. She was smiling. She could feel it. Every part of her body smiled. I have seen heaven and tasted it, she thought to herself, trying to cling to the vapors of her disappearing paradise. The feeling of peace was wonderful, a restful complement to the shimmering fires she had experienced just an instant ago.

She ran her fingertips along his lips, and he kissed each one individually. His eyes now regarded her teasingly. Then he took her in his arms, his breathing gradually becoming more normal, until they both fell asleep.

Morning brought with it light and a prick of common sense to nag at Kate.

"You came, you saw, you conquered," Kate muttered, staring at the muscular outline of the figure lying next to her beneath the crisp chocolate color sheet.

Mike rolled over, not at all asleep, she saw. "You make it sound like a Greek slogan," he said with a grin. "If anyone was conquered last night," he told her fondly, raising his head to kiss the side of her shoulder, "it was me. Miss Sadie Thompson shot an arrow into my heart."

"I'll bet." Kate took a deep breath and tried to push the effect that his naked body was having on her out of the way. "Now what?"

"That depends," Mike said, tugging mischievously at the sheet.

"I mean, how will this affect us in the office?" she pressed.

"Nicely, I hope. Of course, this'll be kind of hard to manage in the office, what with limited space and those short coffee breaks . . ." He yanked down the sheet.

Kate snatched it back. "That's not what I meant," she cried.

Mike's brows knit. "I wasn't planning to paint a scarlet letter on your chest, if that's what you're implying. That wasn't what last night was all about."

"What *was* last night about?" Kate asked.

"Weren't you there?" he teased, running one finger lightly along the upper plane of her breasts. She felt her nipples peaking in response.

"Yes, but—"

She got no further as he began to kiss her ardently again. "It was about a man and a woman getting to know one another very, very well," he whispered huskily.

But she didn't know him, Kate thought later that day after she had come home and evasively fielded Gladys's questions. Fortunately Keith was still asleep. She didn't know Mike at all. All she knew was that she loved being with him. He had aroused her like no other man before him. Although she had finally come to believe that he wasn't out to entrap her, things were still very complicated, very unclear. She still had questions about Gay. And worst of all was the specter of Mike taking his leave in the near future.

She spent a very restless Sunday.

On Monday Kate discovered that Mike was gone. This time his business involved a trip back to the home office in New York, and he would be gone for two weeks. It was an emergency, a brief note to her explained. "Miss me."

Kate did. Two weeks felt like eternity.

She managed to keep herself occupied with work and the remaining performances of *Rain,* but then even that was over. Gladys departed for her monthly jaunt to Las Vegas, and after a final whirlwind tour of downtown Carson City, with a reluctant Kate in tow, Keith headed back for L.A., but not before assuring her that "this one" was a vast improvement over Ryan Kilpatrick ("that turkey"), and that maybe Kate had done a few things right lately—even if she was hanging out in an insurance company, her talent going to waste in local theater. "Remember the *Rain,*" were his last words as he waved to her from the airport runway.

Kate smiled, amused. Remember the *Rain,* indeed. What she remembered these days was the touch of Mike Fleming's hands on her body, the whispered words in her hair, the way he felt pressed close against her, closer than any man had a right to be. "Two people getting to know each other very well"—was that how he'd phrased it? Kate sighed. No, going back to Hollywood for a film career was the last thing on her mind right now.

She drove back from the airport slowly, depressed at the thought of entering her empty house. Too empty, she thought. Another lonely Saturday night. The pile of memos she'd brought home from the office did little to lift her spirits as she sat before the TV set, halfheartedly dispensing with the Icon busywork.

She faced Sunday morning more listlessly than was her custom. It was little consolation that Mike would be home tonight and back in the office tomorrow. Kate tried to interest herself in work, in household chores. Yet none of her normal activities caught her attention even vaguely. Face it, you miss Mike, she told herself, then shook her head ruefully. What would it be like when he was really gone?

He was in New York now, perhaps getting final instructions. The Carson City office had probably "turned around" in New York's eyes: Mike had succeeded. But didn't Carson City need him a little longer? The changes he'd wrought had barely been given time to sink in. Realistically, a new office manager, with a philosophy close to Mike's, could now be sent in and things would undoubtedly run smoothly. Probably Mike's departure *was* imminent. The thought distressed her.

The Sunday paper laid dissected in various corners of the den. An hour dragged by and then another, pulling lethargically at the minutes of the next. Well, cheer up, he's not gone yet, she told herself. After all, he was due to fly in at seven tonight. Seven.

As if in a trance, she looked at the chrome-face clock on her mantel. Five o'clock. If she started now, she could change and be ready to meet his plane. He had mentioned to her which flight he was taking back. She had planned to sit home and wait to see if he called. But maybe...

A smile began to tug at the corners of her mouth, filtering down into her heart. They could have a candlelit dinner and then proceed from there. Her smile grew wider as the thought of spending the night in his arms became more and more vivid. For the first time that day her blood felt as if it was moving in her veins as she went toward her blue-tiled bathroom to shower.

As the steam rose about her, Kate planned what she would wear. Something stylish, she told herself, but tempting, making her appear a cross between a lady and a temptress. A temptress, she added, who was more than willing to deliver. Time was suddenly precious to her. She was going to enjoy what happiness she could grasp.

With one quick turn of the shower dial, she allowed a cascade of cold water to dash about her body, giving her another burst of energy as she fairly leaped out of the stall, toweling herself dry rapidly.

Attired in a becoming peach denim jumpsuit that subtly outlined her supple body, Kate drove to the airport and wound up parking an hour early, anticipation tingling her nerve endings. Tonight was going to be wonderful.

No holding back, no doubts. For the time being she was free of the confining reins of indecision. You make your own happiness, her father had once told her, and she was about to do just that.

Arming herself with a magazine whose title she barely saw, Kate sat down at the designated gate to await the arrival of Mike's plane. She was so engrossed in her plans and in thumbing through the magazine, she didn't know exactly when it was that Gay Ling appeared. But somewhere off in her peripheral line of vision Kate caught a glimpse of an electric blue swatch of silk and a long mane of thick, dark hair that swung about graceful shoulders. Turning, her worst fears were confirmed: Gay Ling, in a designer silk dress that set off the blue highlights in her hair. Gay Ling at her devastating best. So intent was Kate on her scrutiny, and so deep was the stabbing pang that seized her heart, she barely noticed that they were also announcing the descent of Mike's plane.

Now the hurtful pang was mixed with disappointment and anger. What was Gay doing here? Mike had said he wasn't interested in her. Hadn't he found time to mention this to Gay? Trust me, he had said. Trust—what was that?

Kate rose quietly and, as unobtrusively as possible, moved out of the waiting area. She didn't think the Eurasian woman had seen her; Gay's eyes were glued to the window through which the landing plane could be seen. Thinking quickly, Kate sequestered herself behind a series of potted plants that defined the waiting area. From this position she could observe without being seen.

Moments later, as Kate watched Mike traverse the ramp that led to the waiting area, his briefcase under his arm, she felt a burst of regret. Her heart did flip-flops just at the sight of him. But what could she do? Race up to him, just as Gay Ling was doing now—the scene brought a fresh stab of pain to Kate's heart—and grab his other arm? Should she and the exquisite silk-clad woman make this into a tug-of-war, with Mike as the prize? No, that far she wouldn't go. She'd use all her feminine wiles to gain his attention, to consummate their relationship, to win his love. But she wouldn't create a public scene. She wouldn't fight with another woman over him in an airport full of people. That was asking too much.

Kate watched as Gay linked an arm possessively through the crook in Mike's and pressed a warm kiss on his mouth. Whatever investigation Mike was carrying on with Gay had led to just where his investigation of Kate had led, Kate thought grimly. A vivid image of his brown-velvet-covered bed came to her mind. She blinked back her tears. She'd seen enough.

Blindly she made her way back to her car. Shoving a five-dollar bill at the parking attendant and disregarding his shouts about forgetting her change, she sped home.

It served her right, she thought, driving into the empty garage. Falling for a "temporary" man. Of course he'd be playing the field. He wouldn't be sticking around long enough to suffer the consequences of spreading himself so thin. Well, neither would she, she tried to tell herself. Maybe Hollywood did beckon, after all. But for the remainder of his time at Icon—of their time at Icon—it would be strictly business between them.

"Strictly business" lasted until she had the misfortune to be cornered in the walk-in supply closet by Mike early the next morning. Kate, bleary-eyed after a long, sleepless night, had gone in for a work-sheet pad and wound up gazing into Mike's bright green eyes.

"I missed you," he told her softly as they stood together in the cramped space.

How was she going to answer that? Flippantly? Disinterestedly? Or should she kick him in the shin, as she fiercely wanted to do? She decided to answer the best way she knew how—with honesty.

"The hell you did."

"Have I missed something in this conversation?" he asked, lifting her chin to make her look into his eyes.

She glanced toward the door, wondering if anyone would come trooping in in the middle of her tirade. She pulled back behind a row of metal shelves that housed half-open cartons of computer papers and kept her voice low. "When did you have time to miss me? Before or after Gay met your plane?" She pulled her chin from his hand and gathered up the work sheets she used to calculate the monetary values to be paid back on the health claims.

His eyes narrowed. "How did you know about that?"

"You're not the only one carrying on investigations," she said. "I have my ways of getting information."

He shook his head. "I'm not sure I know what you're talking about."

"Neither am I," she mumbled, trying to push past him.

"Gay did meet my plane," Mike began.

"I know," Kate snapped. "I saw."

"You were there?" he asked suddenly, taking her shoulders.

"Right up to the enchanting kiss," she told him, tossing her head for emphasis.

"You came to meet me?" he asked as if he were stuck in first gear.

"No, I like watching planes land. Of course I came," she admitted angrily. "And I felt like a fool for my trouble. I had no idea I would have to contend with other members of the Mike Fleming fan club."

"There is no fan club," he said softly, continuing to block her way. "There's just one overzealous lady who's got her signals crossed."

"Yes, I know. And it's me," she said, wishing she could get out of the tight area. Despite her anger, his nearness was making her weaken.

"No, it's Gay," he told her quite simply. "You're the only one I'm interested in on a personal level."

His sincerity was overwhelming. Delivered in that voice, with that steady gaze, she would have believed it if he told her he'd won the lottery. She blinked her eyes as if to rid herself of the effects of his spell.

"I must be getting back to work," she muttered.

This time he let her go. One of the clerks was entering the supply closet, and she supposed he felt compelled to. Well, it was a good thing, she told herself, taking a deep breath as she headed back to her desk.

So what was she to believe? What her own eyes had told her? Or what Mike had?

Why, why must everything be so hellaciously complicated? She fairly stabbed at her computer as she switched it on.

# CHAPTER
## *Eleven*

THE NEXT WEEK was hectic. The mail had been over-whelming the previous week, and the office was besieged with an astronomical number of health claims. Everyone was doing overtime, and those who caught up were farmed out to help other struggling groups in the office. This cooperative spirit and willingness to work showed Kate— who accepted the evidence grudgingly—just how big a difference Mike had made in the office. But she knew that what was uppermost in his mind was the investi-gation he was conducting covertly. He was still going over personnel files first thing each morning, still calling individuals in for conferences. On the surface it looked as if he were taking a personal interest in each worker, which did wonders for morale. But Kate knew he was still looking for something. What?

She didn't have much time to ponder the question. She had her own work to keep her occupied. Despite the fact that she was a second assistant manager in charge of significant numbers of staff, at times like this she pitched into the tedious work of a regular claims processer with zeal and kept up on her own responsibilities, as well.

For his part, Mike had seemed perfectly willing to abide by the "strictly business" guidelines she had held to herself only with difficulty. His easy acceptance annoyed her, though her common sense told her she should be glad. Meanwhile it helped that she was so busy that she didn't have much time to see him, even on professional issues. Consequently she was informed about the Casbah proposition by Gay Ling.

Gay did not look nearly as harried as the rest of them, Kate thought as the woman lowered herself gracefully into the chair next to Kate's desk. It wasn't Gay's style to assume the duties of her subordinates. Decorum above all, and all that.

"Have you heard about the Casbah account?" the Eurasian woman asked pleasantly.

Kate narrowed her eyes. "No, what about it?"

Gay smiled serenely. "They're thinking of opening a club at Lake Tahoe. That means bigger premiums, possibly different coverage, explaining the package plans—"

"I know what it means," Kate cut in impatiently. "What's the point?"

"The point is," Gay said, leaning forward conspiratorially, "they want Mike and an assistant to come out and talk to the board about it at Las Vegas." She regarded her perfectly manicured nails. "They're offering room and meals, plus entertainment, for free. I think he's going to take me." Her almond-shape eyes shone; she appeared very confident.

"Why you?" Kate asked, forgetting to sound disinterested. "It's my account."

Gay looked at her in surprise, as if the answer was

obvious. "Well, you can't be spared here," she said, gesturing at the work floor. Clerks were filing forms, secretaries typing at a frantic pace. "Everyone knows no one works as fast as you do, and you know so much . . ." Gay let her voice trail off.

"Has Mike appointed you?" Kate asked, her voice hard.

"He's mentioned it," she said vaguely.

Kate rose. "Excuse me, Gay." And with that she marched straight into Mike's office, not caring how it looked to Gay.

Mike looked up from a personnel file, closing it decisively. "To what do I owe this pleasure?" he asked.

"Are you taking Gay Ling to Las Vegas?" Kate asked bluntly, leaning her hands on his desk.

Mike looked bemused for a second before a wide smile graced his lips. "Do I detect jealousy?" he asked, his eyes sparkling devilishly as he rose to come around his desk.

"You detect annoyance," she told him. "I worked on that account."

"I know," he said, "I was there."

"So why does Gay think she's going to Las Vegas with you?"

"Wishful thinking," he said with a shrug. "The reservation is yours if you want it."

"I want it!" she said a little fiercely.

"Good," he replied, and it was apparent to Kate that he was sincere in his display of pleasure.

It deflated her slightly. "It is?" she asked, puzzled. Mike nodded, and Kate felt a little foolish. "I don't understand."

"Okay," he said, sitting down on the edge of his desk and taking her hand. "It's simple." He pointed first to himself and then to her. "Me—you—go—Vegas. Got the picture?"

"No." She withdrew her hand, striving to retain her businesslike demeanor. "I mean, why did Gay say...Did you tell her you were going to take her? As part of your 'investigation,' maybe?" she prodded.

He shook his head. "No, that's not the sort of ploy I'd use. She was in my office when they called. She asked about it; I explained. She wanted to know what would happen if you couldn't come. I said I'd have to take someone else, and she volunteered."

"She would," Kate muttered.

"That's what I've been trying to tell you. Whatever Gay thinks is going on between her and me is strictly in her mind."

Kate let that pass for the moment. "When do we go?" she asked.

"Tomorrow."

"Tomorrow?" she echoed, dumbfounded. "That doesn't give me much time to pack."

"They just called last night. You know how impulsive these show-business types are," he teased.

Kate turned to go.

"Oh, and Kate," he said. She stopped. "Don't pack too much."

The butterflies in her stomach began to flutter once more.

During the plane ride to Las Vegas, Mike provided a steady stream of conversation, touching lightly on everything from the office to his childhood to the arts. She listened in rapt admiration. No wonder he got along so well with people and managed to make the tough New York management board dance to his tune. The tune he played was his own, but it sounded so sweet that the listener was swept away.

Kate had dressed conservatively that morning, knowing the first order of business would be a meeting with

the board of directors at Casbah. She wore a light gray
suit accented by a soft pink blouse with ruffles at the
sleeves and throat. She was the picture of competent
femininity, she felt.

"You look extremely capable," Mike affirmed as they
arrived at the hotel and a valet in a gold uniform rushed
out to whisk the car away. "I'd let you process my claims
any day." This last was murmured into her hair as a gust
of wind brushed several pale strands to his face.

"Fine manager you are." She laughed. "Here we are
minutes away from a meeting involving one of the biggest
accounts Icon has, and all you can think about is sex."

"Yup," he replied, taking her arm. "Must be the company I keep. C'mon, let's get this over with. Then we
can move on to more important matters."

A burst of warmth suffused her body as she followed
Mike into the room.

This time the reception they received was warm. The
personnel manager and his assistant, Amy Lessing, greeted
Kate as though she were an old friend and handled the
introductions all around. When Kate was presented to
one of the vice-presidents, a top entertainer who had been
in the field some thirty years and whose position at Casbah had been created to attract customers, Kate smiled
at him warmly.

"Hi, Eric, how are you?" she said.

The others in the room looked on, obviously wondering how the star would react to being addressed so
familiarly. Soon they had their answer. Eric Eagle hugged
her warmly.

"Little Katie! I can't believe it." He held out her hands
to get a better look at her. "The last time I saw you, your
father was ready to throw you out of the house lock,
stock, and barrel." Smiling broadly, he ran a hand through
his thick white hair.

"And you refereed," she recalled. She looked fondly

at the man who wasn't much taller than she was. "Dad always said you had a silver tongue to go with your golden throat."

"Well, the pipes are still hanging on, Katie." He tapped his broad chest as he slid an arm around her shoulder.

The others looked on curiously. Kate and Eric Eagle exchanged memories for a few moments longer.

"Hey, pardon me," Eric said, looking around at the table. "This is Sean Logan's little girl. All grown up and wheeling and dealing on her own. Whatever she has to sell, buy." He sat down, folding his hands in front of himself and looking very pleased.

Mike laughed. "Well, that might be the quickest sale we ever had. But for the benefit of the others here, I think perhaps you'd like to hear a few of the details."

With that Mike launched into his presentation, yielding the floor to Kate when specifics were called for. Her familiarity with the detailed records enabled her to anticipate problems that might beset the Tahoe-based hotel. The atmosphere in the soft yellow room was warm and friendly, and the presentation went exceptionally well. As Kate glanced at the pictures of celebrities who had graced the old hotel, a sense of well-being washed over her. The portraits, which to others might add glamour, were to her a homey touch. She beamed at Eric Eagle as she drew her remarks to a close, feeling almost relaxed.

"We'll meet in private later on and give you our decision by tomorrow morning," promised the senior vice-president, clasping Mike's hand but including Kate in the scope of his gaze. "It sounds good, mighty good," he assured them. "In the meantime, enjoy yourselves. Everything is on the house."

Considering that when the Salt Lake office had met with the Casbah delegation a little over a year ago, they were made to pay for their own passage and for their rooms as well, Kate took this to be a very good sign.

"See you later, Kate," Eric called. She turned to wave.

"Are there any celebrities you don't know?" Mike asked, a smile tugging his lips. They were ushered to their rooms by a very tall bellboy who wore the costume of a harem eunuch. Everything in the hotel had an old Arabian flavor.

"Tons," Kate said cheerfully. "But my dad's house was a regular clearinghouse for the famous and not-so-famous when I was growing up. It made for a real education," she confided.

The bellboy brought them to the sixth floor. Mike's room was across from Kate's. They retired to their separate quarters to change.

Mike knocked on her door somewhat later. Kate had put on a light dress that cinched in gracefully at the waist and then drifted out, involving yards of skirt that swirled at her slightest movement.

"You're a floating cloud," he said, regarding the violet background and soft lavender flowers.

Kate smiled. "Are you ready to take in the sights?" she asked, closing the door behind her as she stepped out into the hall.

"I think I already am," he said, clasping her hand.

For the rest of the afternoon Kate acted as a guide. Although she had been to Las Vegas many times when she was younger, she had only been back twice since leaving home. Things had changed somewhat, but not so much that she didn't know her way around.

"It's a lot prettier at night," she said. "But you're probably used to Broadway back in New York. The effect is kind of the same, I imagine. Thousands of lights vying for your attention, all trying to outshine one another."

Mike shook his head. "No, even New York's not like this. I've never seen so many light bulbs."

They went to Heldorado Park, where they took their time looking over a collection of authentic stagecoaches, ox carts, and early automobiles. They had planned to go back to the hotel for lunch, but when they passed a Chinese restaurant, they were tempted. Soon they were seated inside.

Almost immediately they were enveloped in the dusky atmosphere. Only an occasional lantern lit the spacious room. A huge fish tank with a collection of colorful tropical fish was in the center; booths and tables encircled the tank. The lanquid action of the fish served to rest the customers' weary eyes.

But Kate and Mike were the only ones there.

After ordering the Businessperson's Special, offering a wide variety of foods, Kate surrendered her menu to the faintly smiling waiter.

"Too bad there aren't three of us," she said to Mike. "Then we'd get egg foo yung as well."

"If madam wants egg foo yung, madam gets egg foo yung," Mike said. He called the waiter back and ordered a side dish for Kate.

The lunch was punctuated with animated conversation. Kate felt as if she'd known him for years. How could she let him simply exit her life? But she never posed the question or allowed it to intrude. They were having too much fun.

They returned to their rooms for a short rest, and then Mike knocked on her door to squire her out for an evening show, a visit to the casinos, and, finally, a late dinner.

In the lobby they ran into Eric Eagle. The singer–cum–senior–vice–president hugged Kate and then gestured at the glass doors, indicating the courtyard outside. "How do you like it?" he asked.

"Looks great," Mike said, taking Kate's hand. They left Eric and went outside together to take a better look. There was a sparkling alabaster fountain in the center of the area. Bathed in multicolored light from a series of floodlights, water cascaded down three tiers to the pool below. The effect was magnificent.

"You know, I feel like a little girl right now," Kate

said wistfully. "I'd love to kick off my shoes and wade in the pool." She put out her hand, letting some of the water splash against it.

"You'd probably drown," Mike said, looking up to see the force with which the water came down from its source twenty feet up. "Besides, you don't look like a little girl." She glanced up and saw herself reflected in his eyes. Her long blue evening dress bared one shoulder entirely as it hugged her breasts. A thin strap kept it up. The shimmering dress enhanced her narrow waist and slim hips as well. A long, daring side slit began at her upper thigh. Her hair was all about her shoulders, loose, the way he liked it.

"You don't look so bad yourself," she said lightly, studying the figure he cut in his custom-made dark blue tuxedo. His ruffled shirt matched her dress.

"Shall we go back inside? The hotel people are probably waiting for us," Mike murmured, putting his arm about her bare back. Just the touch of his hand caused her to shiver involuntarily as she tried once more to deny her need for him.

"Cold?"

"Just a little," she said evasively, quickening her pace.

The well-dressed people at the gaming tables laughed and talked loudly, and the terrific din was all part of the fun. Kate took several turns at the roulette wheel, but on the whole gambling didn't interest her. She found much more excitement in being with Mike, watching women turn their heads as they passed by. She felt she was in heaven.

The Casbah management had gone out of its way to make the evening pleasant. Eric Eagle had reserved them a front table for his eight o'clock show. The singer played the club three times a year, and this, they learned, was opening night. After the show Kate felt it only right that she go backstage and tell her father's old friend just how much they had enjoyed his performance.

"Every performer needs to be told over and over how much he's liked," Kate told Mike as they threaded their way backstage. "It feeds an inner need."

"I didn't know you majored in psychology," Mike said, amused, as the throng pressed against them. A security guard at Eric's dressing room waved the crowds back.

"I'm sorry, miss, but you can't see Mr. Eagle," he told Kate in an impersonal monotone.

"She's okay, kid. He'll want to see her," said the burly man behind Kate. She turned to see the familiar face of one of America's best-loved comedians.

"Jimmy!" she cried. "Jimmy Wales!"

The man chuckled, giving her a hug. "Your dad here?" he asked as he ushered her in.

"No," she said. "I'm here on business. This is my boss." She never let go of Mike's hand.

"Got yourself a great little girl here. I used to change her diapers. I should know." He waggled his shaggy eyebrows. "Except you never looked so good then. Your dad know you dress this way?" he teased. Kate laughed, delighted.

The crowd inside the flower-laden dressing room was so thick that it was hard to move about. Eric Eagle had a lot of well-wishers, all celebrities who had come to see his opening show. Kate quickly tendered her congratulations and her thanks for the tickets, then tried to worm her way back out. Several people recognized her or stopped her because they could not place her face. It felt like old home week with all the people Kate hadn't seen for so long.

"We can stay if you want to," Mike said in a loud voice at the door.

"This isn't any fun for you," she shouted back as the noise grew.

"I'm having fun just watching you," he told her, and she flushed with pleasure.

"C'mon," she said, taking his hand as she went outside. "I'm starved."

Their dinner was served at the terrace restaurant high atop the hotel. It was quite full, but a table by the railing had been reserved for them and a series of potted plants offered them maximum privacy as they ate. Below them was all of Las Vegas, ablaze with light as bright as the overhead stars. In keeping with the hotel's name, the waitresses wore Arabian costumes. Tiny vests topped harem skirts of semisheer material that swished provocatively on slender hips as the women moved. Even the security guards were in costume: they were outfitted as the muscular harem eunuchs who had once guarded the sultan's wives. Curved swords hung at their waists.

"Sure wouldn't want to have a difference of opinion with that one," Mike said, pointing out one who looked like a bona fide giant. "Unless, of course, I had a karate expert present to protect me." He gazed at her significantly.

"You're making fun of me," Kate said, spooning up the last of her dessert.

"I might do a lot of things, but I'd never make fun of you," Mike told her, his voice growing soft. "Is it possible that you grow more beautiful each time I look at you?"

"It's possible that I look better with each glass of wine you have," Kate said with a small smile.

"Why can't you take compliments?"

"I'm not used to them," she said evasively.

"All those celebrities complimented you, and you accepted without turning a hair," he observed.

"That's their way of life," she pointed out. "And the reason they make such a fuss is that when I was little I was an ugly duckling. Keith seemed to have gotten all the looks. I started my awkward teens at the age of six." She took a sip of her coffee and looked down at the city below them. "My mother died shortly after Keith and I were born, you know," she said in a distant voice, "and somehow my father hoped I'd look just like her. It was the least I could have done, in his view," she added, glancing up at Mike again. There was no bitterness in her voice, only sadness. "When it seemed I was slated to be his only homely child, he ignored me in favor of the boys. Perhaps that's why I stopped trying to please him. I'm sure I have him to thank for my independent streak." She blinked, suddenly realizing that she was doing all the talking and that she was baring her soul to him, something she had never done before with anyone. "You do have a way of drawing people out," she said, slightly embarrassed.

"Part of my charm," he told her, his eyes soft. "No one can say you're an ugly duckling anymore."

"Sometimes nature is kind after all," Kate replied. "I finally grew to look like my mother."

They danced to the haunting music of a five-piece orchestra, and Kate found herself thinking that she could go on like this forever, dancing in Mike's arms. But it was getting late, and he looked down, his eyes caressing her face.

"I'd better get you back," he murmured. "We've a meeting with the board at nine, and I want you to get a little rest."

Reluctantly she nodded, and they made their way from the dance floor back to their rooms. There was no one in the halls. The other guests had either retired for the night or were downstairs enjoying the gaming tables and shows.

Kate didn't want the evening to end. She leaned against Mike's shoulder as they walked down the hall. He took her key and opened the door, then handed it back. She was about to say something inane, like what a wonderful evening it had been, when he took her tenderly in his arms and kissed her.

She offered no protest as he pushed her inside and

continued their kiss on the threshold of her room.

"Well, now that you've asked me in..." he said with a trace of mischief. With one hand he closed the door behind him.

Her room was a bedroom from *A Thousand and One Nights*. Earlier she had found it distracting. Now, suddenly, she was grateful. Tall palms decorated the corners, and the bed was the main attraction. It had a canopy that formed a tent, with warm pink and blue veils drifting down from the ceiling and ending at the four corners of the bed. On the bed itself were scattered dozens of little pillows.

"It looks like it's straight out of the *Arabian Nights*, doesn't it?" Kate commented dryly. "Perfect for a harem." She started across the room.

Mike didn't let her get far. Taking hold of her hand, he drew her down onto the king-size comforter with its haunting pattern of multicolor exotic birds. "But I'm no eunuch," he said softly.

His mouth crushed hers with an explosion of passion. His kisses did not stop. Instead they melted her in a barrage of heat that Kate wondered if she could withstand. Once again she felt his hands take possession of her, burning a path along her body everywhere he touched. Soon she was lying on the bed with Mike's body against hers, making her forget who she was and where she was, everything but her crying need for his love, his wanting of her.

"I need you, Kate. I need you," he whispered over and over again, his breath enveloping her, fanning the fire within her yearning body.

"Yes," she cried, "yes," as his exploring fingers roused all her smoldering emotions.

She hardly heard the knock on the door, for her head was filled with the sound of his breathing, but Mike's head was up, alert.

"Katie, Katie, are you in there?" came the familiar

voice, accompanied by a light staccato rapping.

Dazed, Kate shook her head, hugely sad suddenly at what had almost happened—and hadn't.

"Better answer that," Mike said, rezipping her dress in the back and gently pushing her shoulder strap back up. She looked at him. His face was a mask of control.

"Katie?"

Kate rose and opened the door. Keith stood in her doorway, a winsome girl on his arm. He took a look inside, and his chagrin was instantly apparent. "Gee, I didn't mean to interrupt anything," he apologized. "But Eric told me you were staying here and I thought I'd pop by. I came for his late show. This is Janie," he added almost lamely, nodding to the lovely redhead.

Kate smiled, trying to look happy to see them. Normally she would have been delighted. But right now . . . delight had floated away on winged feet. "We're only here until tomorrow morning. Come on in," she said, gesturing toward the room. Mike came to the door and stood behind her.

"No, no, I'll catch you later. I think I've done enough damage for one night," he whispered in her ear as he bent to kiss her forehead. "Gladys will be very happy."

"There's nothing to be happy about," Kate whispered back. But already he was walking away, his friend in tow.

Kate turned around and looked at Mike. "Are you going to leave?" she asked.

He ran his finger along the line of her chin. "Do you want me to?"

"No," she replied, unable to help herself. She searched his face to see if her honesty had put him off. There was no sign of it in his eyes.

"Good," he said, drawing her into his arms once again. "I don't want to go." He kissed the point of her shoulder ever so lightly, making wonderful things happen to her. "All evening long, all I could think of was kissing every inch of your body, starting at your toes and working my way up."

"You've got your directions confused," she managed to murmur, the mental image generated by his words exciting her. "That's my shoulder."

"I take opportunity where I find it." His hand was already pressing the long zipper against her spine, slipping it lower and lower, parting the material from her body and leaving her free for his all-consuming gaze.

He picked her up and gently placed her in the center of the elaborate bed, joining her before she even had time to lift her arms to him. His clothes had melted away in the mists that seemed to surround her. He was weaving his web of passion well, she thought distantly as his hands once more took possession of what was clearly his, caressing the smooth, eager skin that presented itself to him. But this time, Kate thought, this time she didn't want to be just the overwhelmed recipient of his lovemaking. She wanted to be an active partner, to make him want her again and again, so that he was as fiercely in need of her loving as she found she was of his.

With eager fingers she kneaded a pattern along his strong back, her cool hands stroking the long expanse downward, pulling him closer as she let loose the passion he had caused to swell within her.

This time there was no attempt to hold back. Everything she was, Kate allowed to come forth. The competent, efficient Kate Lonigan was left somewhere by the wayside as Kate the passionate woman emerged to take her place, matching kiss for rapturous kiss.

She continued to explore Mike's body with hands that were no longer hesitant at their task. The touch of his sinewy flesh made her feel closer to him than she had before, and she could see that her light, fluttering touch excited him. A low, satisfied moan escaped his lips. Raw desire shone in his eyes.

"Oh Kate, Kate," he murmured as she bent her head

to press her lips at the side of his neck. She could feel the vibration of his vocal cords as he spoke. More, she could feel the effect of her probing fingers by the way he moved against her, the hardening contours of his body growing more demanding as her hand became acquainted with the intimate haven.

They clung to one another in a sea of ecstasy, moving rhythmically with more and more force. It was as if they were being fused together, as if they had been created as one since the beginning of time. And then, finally, it was over, peace bursting upon Kate with as much force as the heat of passion had before.

She sighed deeply, cradled in his arms. She could feel the downy hair upon his arm as it lay near her breast. The sensation was exquisite.

"Hey, you're some tigress," he whispered against her ear, his free hand tracing the outline of her face as if he were willing his fingers to memorize the features.

He raised himself on one elbow, looking unabashedly at her naked form.

"Anything wrong?" she asked, her voice low.

"No, everything's perfect," he told her, his hand now gliding down the plane of her throat, then whisking across first one breast and then another. His motion caused the veins in her breasts to tingle with excitement and her nipples to grow hard. "Absolutely perfect," he repeated, his voice barely audible as he lowered his head to kiss the place where his hands had been a moment before.

Kate entwined her fingers in his thick dark hair, holding him even closer as she felt the now-familiar ardor beginning to rise again. Moaning softly, she began to sway once again, her body rubbing against the downy network of the light hairs upon his chest.

The night slipped away into timelessness, and sleep was something that came only in the very wee hours of the morning.

\*   \*   \*

Kate's wake-up call broke into the peaceful blanket of sleep that had overtaken her. As the shrill ringing persisted, she pried open her eyes to find Mike groping for the phone.

"Mmm?" were the only words he seemed to be able to manage. But then he sat up, alert. Business did that to him, Kate thought, gingerly allowing herself to feel the length of his manly body next to hers. She wondered if he noticed that she had pressed her thigh against his.

He noticed, she realized, as he hung up and with just one "Good morning" began to pick up where he had left off the night before.

"Aren't we late?" she protested.

"We're the stars," he told her, kissing the hollow of her throat and driving her crazy. "They'll hold the curtain for us."

It was all the argument she needed.

When they arrived at the meeting only ten minutes late, thanks to a reluctant eye kept on the bedside clock, they were greeted warmly. Over steaming mugs of coffee and crisp croissants, they learned the good news: their presentation had gone over well. Icon Carson City would be awarded the lucrative Casbah contract.

Kate's elation was palpable. It was all she could do not to reach over and kiss Mike. But he was all business, she saw as she admired his strong profile. Somehow this endeared him to her the more. She knew that alone in bed at night, he was all hers. She smiled.

Their flight left at eleven, and by early afternoon they were back in the Carson City office, facing a new crisis. The head of Nevada Medical Supplies was on the premises and threatening to pull his entire account from Icon, a worried receptionist informed them. Kate lifted her head. Jack Bristol's powerful voice could be heard booming through the walls of Dave's office even though the door was closed. Mike and Kate exchanged glances, and Mike headed for the door. Kate followed. It hadn't occurred to her to hang back or leave this matter to him.

Dave's face showed its relief visibly when his boss entered.

"Mr. Bristol," said Mike smoothly, shaking the gaunt man's hand. "What seems to be the problem?" He seated himself on the edge of the desk, looking at the red-faced corporate president in a friendly manner.

"The problem is you've got a bunch of idiots running this office, that's what the problem is! And I came in personally to tell you so. Look at this!" He waved a memo in front of Mike's face. It was a standard office memo used by the processors to deny a claim. The missive denied Jack Bristol's claim because there was no record of his being an employee of Nevada Medical Supplies. It was signed by Gay Ling.

Mike gave Dave a sharp look. "Where's Gay?" he asked.

"She took the day off," Dave grumbled.

Angrily Mike buzzed for Gay's assistant. When the heavyset, obviously nervous young woman arrived, he instructed Kate to take her into his office to discuss the matter in private. When they had shut the door behind them, Kate showed the woman the denial form. "Do you have any idea how this happened?" she asked.

The woman shook her head nervously, one hand twisting at the belt on her skirt.

"Don't you have a microfiche from the home office?" Kate asked. The New York office regularly issued a complete listing of all the covered employees on microfiche cards.

"Ms. Ling has one," the woman volunteered.

They went to Gay's desk and found the microfiche, but a perusal of the listing found it indeed wanting. The company president's name was not on it.

"What do you do when you don't find a name on this?" Kate asked patiently.

"We deny the claim," the girl said hesitantly. "Gay told us to."

"You don't call the company?" Kate asked incredulously, wondering why standard procedure was ignored. "Personnel?"

The woman shook her head. "No, only Ms. Ling talks to them. She said that half the employees didn't pay their health insurance premiums. They just mailed their claims in, hoping to get paid. She told us to go with the microfiche listing and she would take care of any problems."

"I see," Kate said, taking a deep breath. Mike was going to have to do a lot of smooth talking, she thought, glancing at the door to his office.

Jack Bristol looked a little more in control of himself when Kate returned. She excused herself and took Mike aside, telling him what she had found out as quickly as possible. She could see his jaw tighten as he kept his anger in check. Kate knew by now that nothing irritated Mike more than flagrant incompetence.

"Mr. Bristol, I'm afraid you're the victim of a computer error. I promise you that we'll have everything squared away for you within the next few days."

"Well, it's not just me," Bristol said. "I understand that a number of my employees have complained. I thought you people ran a tight ship here."

"Some of the rigging came loose, I'm afraid," Mike said dryly, looking toward Gay's area. Her Out box was piled high with folders and claims she had supposedly audited. "But if you'll only give us a few more days, I give you my word that you'll be back on an even keel," he said, extending the metaphor.

"Well." The man shrugged. "I guess we'll take your word for it. *This* time," he emphasized, rising. "I went to bat for you with our board a few months back. I'd sure hate to be standing there with egg on my face."

"No egg, I promise," Mike said, extending his hand.

He walked Bristol to the outer door.

Kate glanced at the clock. It was past two on a Friday afternoon. This was not the time to start a rush project. She could see the restlessness beginning to build as the first shift waited for their three o'clock quitting time.

"What are you planning to do?" Kate asked as Mike walked back in through the door. Dave had left for a dental appointment.

"Those claims have to be checked, for openers," Mike said, making his way to Gay's desk. Four additional stacks stood in the back of her cubicle, each about a foot and a half high. All the folders were thin, Kate noted hopelessly.

"All of them," she murmured, disheartened. She could read the look in Mike's eyes.

"Get a file boy to box them up for us," Mike told her, riffling through Gay's desk, looking for the coverage information.

"Where are you taking them?" she asked.

"Home," he told her.

"You know how to work claims?" she asked in surprise.

"Of course," he said. "I told you. When I run an office, I run it." He glared down at the stacks. "I don't buy the prima-donna theory of management," he added. "Hope you weren't planning anything this weekend."

"Why?" she asked suspiciously.

"Because you're going to help."

Kate looked at the stacks and sighed.

# CHAPTER
# *Twelve*

KATE SAT BACK on her heels, crouched before the file cabinet in Gay's cubicle. Something was wrong. Perhaps knowing Mike had been sent to Carson City to "investigate" something made her more alert to the goings-on in the office, even though she had no idea what the subject of his investigation was. But this new element was unusual enough to disturb her. It just didn't feel right. She sighed, standing up.

After Mike's dictum she had decided to stay late at the office. Most of Gay's files had already been boxed and sent to Mike's home. But the Nevada Medical file, which Kate had kept out, remained, and she was checking through it now, going back and forth from the folders to the microfiche employee list on Gay's desk. And something didn't jibe.

Eligibility of a claimant, Kate knew, was established by locating the name on the microfiche to determine if he or she was listed and when coverage had begun. The microfiche list was frequently inaccurate. Therefore, if a person wasn't listed, standard procedure was to place a call to the company's personnel office to see if there had been an oversight.

In the Nevada Medical Supplies account, only one employee was listed in the claims file who was not listed on the microfiche.

Checking further, Kate saw that on matters regarding this claimant—Simone Pensworth—there had been no verifying calls made, for that information was ordinarily noted on the front of the file. The claim, unlike any of the others for Nevada Medical Supplies, had been handled personally by Gay. It was easy to recognize her baroque, curlicued script. Indeed, Kate now saw, paging through the Pensworth folder, Gay had handled all the claims submitted by this employee. There were quite a few.

Kate decided to check it out. Dialing personnel at Nevada Medical, she found the switchboard was closed. She checked her watch. Of course. It was after five on a Friday; she'd been so engrossed that she'd lost track of time. Frowning, she made a note on her memo pad to call first thing Monday morning. Back in her own office, she noted this on her calendar, and at last she was ready to leave.

She arrived at Mike's house at seven Saturday morning, wearing jeans and a T-shirt that proclaimed: They can't fire me, slaves have to be sold. Mike laughed when he saw it. He ushered her into his den. The spacious room caught a lot more of the morning light than his living room did, making it easier to work.

"Very appropriate, Kate. Sit down and grab a claim. The coverage documents are over there." He pointed to the corner of his massive desk.

"One question," Kate asked as she pulled up a chair

near him. "Why are *we* doing this?"

"It's not to save Gay's name, if that's what you're thinking," Mike told her. "I just don't want our reputation undermined by such gross negligence. And no one below assistant management is authorized to check these. I don't think we can expect Milt to do it. He's a decent worker, but he's as slow as molasses. You're fast," he told her. "At least in terms of work." There was a twinkle in his eye.

Kate debated telling him about her discovery. Perhaps she was blowing something out of proportion. She decided to keep her silence for a while. Marguerite, whose day off this was, had laid out sandwiches for them before she left. Kate nibbled as she worked. Every once in a while she caught herself glancing up in Mike's direction. He was totally absorbed in the task at hand, so different today from the passionate man who had stirred her to unimagined heights just two nights ago! Now he was all business, determined to salvage an important account for the company.

"A penny for your thoughts," he said, looking up suddenly to catch her staring.

She shook her head. "Sorry, inflation has eaten away at your penny. The price is now a quarter."

"How about a kiss?" Mike asked, moving in closer. Kate was sitting tailor-fashion on the floor, surrounded by claims, and she saw it was no easy task for him to pick his way toward her. "That might be worth a quarter."

He bent his head. Kate clamped her arms about his neck, almost making him fall as she pulled him in, laughing. "Much more," she said as he unceremoniously joined her on the floor.

"Need a break?" he asked, cocking his head invitingly.

She knew what he had in mind. "If we start that, we'll never finish all this." But her protest carried little conviction as a delicious tingle of anticipation began to filter its way through her body.

"Somehow," he said, taking a file from her hands, "I can't keep my hands on my work anymore. What do you suggest I do about it?"

"Seize opportunity where you may," she said, recalling his words and hoping he would do just that.

And he did.

But then the clock in the hall chimed out that another hour had flitted by and Mike raised himself off the sofa, shrugging back into his shirt, watching Kate slip on her clothing. "If it weren't for this damned mess, I'd have locked up your clothes and kept you prisoner all night."

"Promises, promises." Kate laughed. "C'mon," she said with resignation, looking back at the piles on the floor. "Icon calls us back to duty."

Between the two of them they managed to get the bulk of the work ready for computer input.

"And you've already checked them against the microfiche?" he asked.

She nodded in response and thought of the one odd file.

"That's a strange look you just gave me. What's the matter? Did the perfect employee forget that step?" he teased.

They were sitting on the sofa, sharing a glass of wine, toasting themselves on a job well done. The sun was turning a bright gold outside the patio window, but Kate's mind was now firmly focused on the file. Was she making a mountain out of the proverbial molehill? She wouldn't have made the discovery if she hadn't for some reason decided to check backward from the microfiche to the file. And even then it might not have struck her if she hadn't noticed Gay's handwriting. Was her dislike of Gay the reason for her suspicion?

"Come on, out with it," Mike coaxed.

And so she told him. She had half-expected him to laugh off her suspicions as melodramatic. Her other half had expected to be teased for pettiness or jealousy. Instead Mike jumped up, startled. When he looked down at her, his expression was serious. "Let me see that file," he said.

She had just gone over it; it was right at the top of the stack. On the surface the charges had looked all right. Kate handed Mike the file.

He looked it over carefully before he glanced back at her. "I don't want you telling anyone else about this, okay?"

"Why?" she wanted to know. "Does this have anything to do with your investigation?"

"It might."

"You're beginning to sound like James Bond. Look," she said, slightly exasperated, "I found the file. The least you can do is tell me what I found."

"Maybe nothing," Mike said. But she doubted it. "I want you to call personnel at Nevada Medical first thing Monday morning and let me know immediately what you find out."

"I'd already planned to do that," she said, still thinking that the whole thing was strange. And she was annoyed that Mike woudn't confide in her. He had made love to her in two different cities! Didn't he trust her yet? Not with the company secrets, apparently. She pursed her lips.

"Hey, don't look so annoyed," Mike said, kissing her temple as he escorted her back to her car. He'd already pleaded an overload of work for the rest of the weekend, and Kate, although she was thrilled to have spent so much time with him in Las Vegas and after, was glad for the break. She needed a quiet Saturday night and Sunday to herself. His absence didn't bother her, but his lack of trust most certainly did. "I'll explain everything the moment I can. It's probably nothing," he continued persuasively.

But although Kate gave him the smile he seemed to want, she knew it wasn't "nothing" that made him look so pensive. She pulled away, glancing into her rearview mirror. Mike stood in the driveway, looking after her.

Monday morning the sky threatened to let rain engulf the city in one of those famous desert storms. It had only begun to sprinkle when Kate left, but the gray clouds that all but blocked the sun were clearly swollen with rain. Kate entered the office to see Mike and one of the file boys dragging a dolly loaded down with the boxed claims. He flashed her an appreciative smile.

Mike glanced at his watch as he passed her. "Try calling them at eight-thirty," he advised without any preamble. Kate knew that the matter of the odd file hadn't left his mind since Saturday.

At eight-thirty she was on the phone, calling Nevada Medical Supplies. There would be no one there until nine, she was informed by a nasal recording.

At nine Gay arrived, wearing a dress that crossed the fine line between being chic office wear and being blatantly sexy. Kate glanced at the low-cut front, a little surprised. Gay was usually carefully professional in appearance. Kate wondered if the dress was for Mike's benefit. She glanced down at her own wraparound skirt and gray blouse and felt almost dowdy.

Determinedly she reached for the phone again. This time she was connected with a woman from personnel, and she asked for the eligibility date of one Simone T. Pensworth. After being put on hold for ten minutes, Kate was rewarded with the answer that there was no eligibility date—because there was no such employee.

"Are you sure?" Kate asked, staring at the file in front of her. "Maybe we've got it down wrong. Maybe it's Simone's husband, Arthur, who's the employee."

But no Arthur Pensworth worked for Nevada Medical Supplies, either.

"Thank you very much," Kate managed to mumble, then hung up, confused. According to what she saw in the file, Simone Pensworth had been with the company for several years. She had run up a number of heavy medical claims recently, as had her husband, although each check that had been issued was under the $5,000 limit that would trigger an automatic audit. Kate was chewing pensively on her pencil when her phone buzzed.

"Kate?" It was Mike's voice.

"There is no Simone Pensworth," she said slowly, still allowing the consequences of her discovery to sink in.

"Are you sure?" he asked, his voice tense.

"I just got off the phone with the personnel department. The woman was very thorough."

"I'll be by in a minute to get the file. Don't say anything," he cautioned.

Mike's face was grave when he came for the file. But he gave Kate no further information and simply asked that she continue to work on the other files for him. The directive bothered her. After all, Gay was back. Why wasn't *she* being told to handle them? It was her work.

But she sighed and did as she was told, spending the rest of the afternoon hard at work, sorting through Gay's files. All her suspicions about the woman, built up over the months, were now confirmed, she thought grimly. Gay did as little work as she could get by with. Her claims files had been one disorganized, incompetent mess—until Mike and she undertook to straighten them out.

At noon Kate approached Mike's office, needing his opinion on one of the claims. To her surprise, his office was dark.

"He's not in," his secretary, a plump woman named Sally, told Kate, who was already reaching for the light switch.

"So I see," said Kate, puzzled. "Where is he?" She didn't think he had had any meetings scheduled for today.

"He took Ms. Ling out to lunch," Sally said, glancing at the notation on her calendar as she continued to type Mike's letter to the microfiche department.

Kate froze in her tracks. "Are you sure?" she asked quietly.

"That's what he told me," Sally said. "Said he'd be gone awhile."

"I see," Kate replied, pressing her lips together. She clenched her hands against her sides so hard she could feel her nails digging into her palms as she walked away.

He was lunching Gay at some restaurant, while Kate stayed in and did Gay's work. It was an outrage! Gay's new dress had probably done the trick, she fumed as she walked back to her desk. Sitting, she tried to calm herself down.

She didn't succeed. As time went on and Mike didn't reappear, Kate became more and more incensed. She realized now that in all likelihood Gay had made up the Pensworth family in order to collect on their claims. Granted, Gay did live alone and had no one else to take care of. But the car she drove was an expensive one, and her designer clothes undoubtedly cost a bundle. Gay was embezzling funds from Icon! And from all appearances, despite Mike's protests to the contrary, she had apparently seduced him into looking the other way. You didn't take embezzlers out to lunch! How Gay had managed this coup, Kate could only guess. And didn't want to, she thought grimly. An image of Gay in her low-cut dress sprang vividly to mind.

By two-thirty they had not returned. Kate couldn't take being in the office a moment longer. Telling the secretary she was sick, she left.

"What are you doing here?" Gladys called in surprise as Kate came in. She glanced at her watch and shook it to see if it was running. Kate was never home early.

Kate couldn't find the words to answer. Outside the rumble of thunder could be heard. The storm was finally breaking. Well, Kate couldn't care less.

"Hey, kid, what's the matter? You sick or something?" Gladys asked, coming toward her from the kitchen. She reached out to feel her forehead. "You look terrible."

Kate shook her head. "I'm just keyed up, that's all. Any coffee?" She knew Gladys always kept a pot on during the day.

"Help yourself," Gladys said, indicating the pot on the stove, then thought better of it. "No, here, let me get it for you. You sit down."

"I'm all right, Gladys," Kate insisted, doing as the woman said.

"Here, kid, drink it down." Gladys was pressing a cup of hot black coffee into her hands. "There's a chill out."

There was a chill in, too, Kate thought, a strong chill. She downed the hot black liquid in four gulps.

"Where are you going?" Gladys demanded.

"Out," she snapped as she closed the door behind her.

Within five minutes the downpour came.

Kate was wet and miserable when she returned an hour later, but at least her thoughts were channeled to practical matters. Like getting out of her wet clothes. She began to unlock the door, pushing her soaking hair from her face, when the door gave way and swung open. She looked up into Mike's glaring face. Never had she seen him so angry.

"Where the hell have you been?" he demanded, pulling her into her house.

"Out," she snapped. "Walking. What are *you* doing here? Did you find more of Gay's claims for me to do?"

"You look like a drowned rat," he told her, anger

warring with concern in his voice.

"Thanks for the compliment. Now would you please get out of here?"

"Let me help you out of those wet clothes," he said.

"Oh, no!" Kate raised her hands to ward him off. "I'll keep my clothes on and my sensibilities intact, thank you. Keep your hands off, you hear?" Then she saw that Gladys was standing by, taking it all in. "Gladys, please leave—no, stay!" she cried, changing her mind as she saw Mike's expression.

But Gladys was already reaching into the hall closet for her coat and purse. "I'm going where it's less noisy," she declared. "Like to a war movie." She slammed out before Kate could stop her.

"Now will you tell me what this is all about?" Mike demanded. Kate stomped away from him, her shoes sloshing. She hurried toward her bedroom. He was quick to follow.

"Why should I tell you anything? You're the one who thrives on secrets!"

"Are you deranged? Now cut it out and talk to me!" Grabbing her arms, he swung her around.

"You're protecting Gay Ling, aren't you." It was a statement, not a question.

"No," he said flatly.

"Do you always take the people you're 'investigating' out to eat?" She glared at him.

"Eat?" he asked incredulously.

"Lunch. You bought Gay Ling lunch."

"What?" A slow smile of understanding was spreading over Mike's face. It only made Kate more furious. Now he was mocking her.

"Lunch? Who told you that? I fired her."

"You—you what?"

"Fired her. And then I had to go to the U.S. attorney's office and swear out an affidavit. She's bilked Icon out of thousands of dollars." A look of weariness descended over his face. "Kate," he said, "I guess it's time I explained a few things." He looked at her, then seemed to notice her shivering for the first time. Her clothes were plastered against her body, revealing every detail. "You're going to catch your death if you don't take those things off," he said, moving over to close her bedroom window. Outside the desert storm had stopped as quickly as it began.

"First of all," he continued, "I want you to get one thing through that lovely head of yours. No matter what it's looked like on the surface, I haven't touched another woman since I met you. I haven't wanted to," he added softly.

"Not even Gay Ling?" she asked, feeling the need to be specific. If course, he could be lying. But it was harder to lie to a direct question.

"Least of all Gay," he told her, and his eyes never wavered. He began to unbutton her wet blouse.

Kate trembled as his fingers continued their work. "See, you're catching cold already," he told her, stripping the blouse off. One quick movement of the wrist and her wet wraparound skirt fell to the floor. She stood before him in soft pink undergarments that clung damply to her body. He pulled her close.

"You'll get wet, too," she protested weakly.

"I don't care if I get pneumonia," he said, kissing her upturned mouth. The flame that burst within her dried her faster than even the sun could have. Behind her she felt Mike release the hook of her bra. Slowly he pulled down the straps, first from one shoulder and then another, not lifting his lips from hers till the dainty garment fell to the floor beside her skirt.

Her breath grew shorter as she was pushed gently backward. Mike had stripped the bed of its warm cover, and now he wrapped the quilt around her.

"I don't want you freezing to death. No matter how much I'd rather see you naked."

But she rose from the spot where he'd set her, the quilt draped about her shoulders; it slipped as she approached him, till it was on the floor as well. Mike did not take his eyes from hers as she opened his shirt with trembling fingers. He made no move to help her.

Her eyes never leaving his face, she unhooked his belt. Within a moment he was out of his clothes, standing before her, ready for her love. She caught her breath, afraid to give in to her passions, become vulnerable— and afraid not to.

But he gave her no time to think. His eyes were filled with love as he lifted her onto the bed. His hands slid beneath her silken panties to slip them from her hips in rhythmic motions as he kissed her over and over again, pressing his burning flesh to hers.

At last Kate allowed herself to be consumed by her desires. She knew no restraint. Her heart pounded in her ears as she pulled him closer and closer, feeling that they would never be close enough and that the need within her would never, ever be satisfied.

She arched her back against his hard, muscular frame, wanting to feel every inch of him against her, loving the fire between them. His lips descended the now-familiar path to her breasts, teasing, nibbling, whipping her frenzy to new heights as his hands caressed her softness, making her his over and over again.

As the swirling heat inside her reached a crescendo, a whisper of ecstasy escaped Kate's lips. Mike drove her body harder against the soft comforter, making her forget any questions that still lay unanswered.

# CHAPTER
## *Thirteen*

"So now are you going to explain?" Kate asked.

An hour had passed. The rain had left heavy tracks on her bedroom window, and the light sound of an occasional wayward drop could still be heard plinking against the pane. Inside things were far rosier, with only the muted light from one hurricane lamp to illuminate them. Kate surrendered her warm place nestled against Mike's chest to look him directly in the eye.

"I thought I had," he teased.

"The details," she said, poking a playful finger against his chest. "And please be complete. Start at the beginning . . ."

"The beginning?" Mike scratched his head. "Well, let's see. I was sent to investigate the truth about a rumor—an accusation, really."

Kate knew he was drawing this out to tease her. "Which was?" she prodded.

"The president got a letter from an anonymous source

**177**

saying that someone in the Carson City office was embezzling funds. He thought it was probably some crank playing a joke, but every hint of wrongdoing of that magnitude must be looked into."

"And so he sent you," Kate concluded. She toyed with her hair a bit forlornly. The mystery was solved now. He would be leaving. Pain stabbed through her heart. But she wouldn't dwell. Time enough for that later. "Did you suspect me?" she asked.

"I suspected everyone," he told her honestly. "And what better candidate than someone with a house and a housekeeper on a second assistant's salary?" He grinned.

"Little did you realize that I was just a poor little rich girl in disguise," she said, batting her eyes and rolling them for effect.

He put his arms about her, pulling her close. "Woman," he corrected. "A smoldering, passionate woman. You ruled yourself out for good when you told me who you really were, who your family was." He paused a moment to lift a strand of her hair and set it back gently on her forehead. "By then," he told her, "we were turning up some irregularities in accounting. I met individually with every employee at Icon. But the trail kept leading back to Gay."

"So I noticed," she said with a smile. She could feel his heart beating against her breast. What a wonderful, secure feeling. But how long would it last?

"It was strictly business," Mike said innocently.

"Uh-huh, and I know just how you operate." She ran her finger along his lips.

"No, that technique was reserved for you alone," he said. She would have liked to believe he was sincere. "But on with my story, since you're so eager to hear it. I was suspicious about the, ah—furnishings Gay could afford on her salary—"

"So, what's her bedroom like?" Kate asked.

"Wouldn't know," Mike countered without skipping a beat, and Kate laughed.

"You're quick," she conceded.

"I have to be. Look who I'm up against." Fondly he kissed her chin. "Anyway, I had nothing concrete until you found that Nevada Medical folder. Apparently she had arranged that the money be sent to a post-office box in South Tahoe. She'd set up an account in the Pensworths' name at the local bank there. But it was only one of several different accounts in different locations."

Kate shook her head. "No wonder she did so little work here and took so much time off. She had her hands full." She sighed, still somewhat stunned. "So what happens to her now?"

"It's out of my hands," Mike told her. "Insurance fraud is a federal offense."

"Somehow," Kate said thoughtfully, "I'll bet Gay will charm her way out of this. She'll give a great performance on the stand. She'll wind up with a hand slapping, a suspended sentence, and a dinner out with her rich attorney. Wanna bet?"

"No," Mike told her, grabbing her hand. "I only bet on sure things."

"Like your leaving?" Kate asked in a quiet voice.

"Leaving? Who said anything about that?"

"Well, your mission is over. Icon's funds are intact. The Carson City branch is running like a dream. Isn't it time for you to ride off into the sunset?"

"That's west," he told her. "Icon's in New York—east."

"Whatever," she mumbled, not feeling nearly as cheerful as she had moments earlier.

"Well, if this is the brush-off, lady, you sure picked a hell of a time to do it: when I'm in bed with my pants down." He looked at her more closely. "What would you say if I told you I was thinking of staying on?"

Kate brightened instantly, but she tried to play down her elation. Was this another tease? "I'd say that was nice," she said casually.

"Just nice?"

She took in a deep breath, trying not to look at him. "I'd say a lot of things. But they would give away how I feel."

"How *do* you feel?" he asked tenderly.

"Is this another verbal questionnaire?" she asked, allowing the trace of a smile.

"Well, why not?" Mike asked. "Just think of it as a new investigation."

Kate groaned. "What's the subject of this one?"

"Oh, haven't I told you?" he asked, a smile tugging at the corners of his mouth. His tone was serious, though. "A brand-new position opened up recently, one I never dreamed would need filling."

"And the title is?" Kate asked, only half-interested. Work faded in importance whenever she was in bed with him.

"Mrs. Michael Fleming," he told her simply.

Kate's eyes grew large as his words sank in. Her mouth felt dry and she swallowed before she ventured to ask, "And the requirements?"

"The successful applicant will be someone quite extraordinary. She will have a rare sense of humor. And a level head in any crisis," he added significantly. Kate knew he was referring to her recent suspicions over him and Gay, teasing her. "A good complexion and sound teeth wouldn't be bad, either." He stroked her cheek.

"Able to leap tall buildings in a single bound?" she asked, sitting up against her floral pillow. The sheet slipped from her breasts and Mike's gaze shifted with it.

"Only in emergencies," he murmured, cupping her breasts gently. He kissed first one, then the other, sending slings of fiery arrows raging through her. "The most important requirement is that she love me," he said, looking into her eyes. His own expression was momentarily serious.

"She does," Kate whispered. "She does very much."

Mike pulled her back down on top of him, and she felt the hot imprint of his body against hers as he kissed her lips over and over. "That's good," he managed huskily. "I would hate for it to be all one-sided."

"That could never happen," Kate murmured against his mouth as his lips took possession of her, body and soul. "That could never happen."

_____ 06864-0 **A PROMISE TO CHERISH** #100 LaVyrle Spencer

_____ 06866-7 **BELOVED STRANGER** #102 Michelle Roland

_____ 06867-5 **ENTHRALLED** #103 Ann Cristy

_____ 06869-1 **DEFIANT MISTRESS** #105 Anne Devon

_____ 06870-5 **RELENTLESS DESIRE** #106 Sandra Brown

_____ 06871-3 **SCENES FROM THE HEART** #107 Marie Charles

_____ 06872-1 **SPRING FEVER** #108 Simone Hadary

_____ 06873-X **IN THE ARMS OF A STRANGER** #109 Deborah Joyce

_____ 06874-8 **TAKEN BY STORM** #110 Kay Robbins

_____ 06899-3 **THE ARDENT PROTECTOR** #111 Amanda Kent

_____ 07200-1 **A LASTING TREASURE** #112 Cally Hughes $1.95

_____ 07203-6 **COME WINTER'S END** #115 Claire Evans $1.95

_____ 07212-5 **SONG FOR A LIFETIME** #124 Mary Haskell $1.95

_____ 07213-3 **HIDDEN DREAMS** #125 Johanna Phillips $1.95

_____ 07214-1 **LONGING UNVEILED** #126 Meredith Kingston $1.95

_____ 07215-X **JADE TIDE** #127 Jena Hunt $1.95

_____ 07216-8 **THE MARRYING KIND** #128 Jocelyn Day $1.95

_____ 07217-6 **CONQUERING EMBRACE** #129 Ariel Tierney $1.95

_____ 07218-4 **ELUSIVE DAWN** #130 Kay Robbins $1.95

_____ 07219-2 **ON WINGS OF PASSION** #131 Beth Brookes $1.95

_____ 07220-6 **WITH NO REGRETS** #132 Nuria Wood $1.95

_____ 07221-4 **CHERISHED MOMENTS** #133 Sarah Ashley $1.95

_____ 07222-2 **PARISIAN NIGHTS** #134 Susanna Collins $1.95

_____ 07233-0 **GOLDEN ILLUSIONS** #135 Sarah Crewe $1.95

_____ 07224-9 **ENTWINED DESTINIES** #136 Rachel Wayne $1.95

_____ 07225-7 **TEMPTATION'S KISS** #137 Sandra Brown $1.95

_____ 07226-5 **SOUTHERN PLEASURES** #138 Daisy Logan $1.95

_____ 07227-3 **FORBIDDEN MELODY** #139 Nicola Andrews $1.95

_____ 07228-1 **INNOCENT SEDUCTION** #140 Cally Hughes $1.95

_____ 07229-X **SEASON OF DESIRE** #141 Jan Mathews $1.95

_____ 07230-3 **HEARTS DIVIDED** #142 Francine Rivers $1.95

_____ 07231-1 **A SPLENDID OBSESSION** #143 Francesca Sinclaire $1.95

_____ 07232-X **REACH FOR TOMORROW** #144 Mary Haskell $1.95

_____ 07233-8 **CLAIMED BY RAPTURE** #145 Marie Charles $1.95

_____ 07234-6 **A TASTE FOR LOVING** #146 Frances Davies $1.95

_____ 07235-4 **PROUD POSSESSION** #147 Jena Hunt $1.95

All of the above titles are $1.75 per copy except where noted

---

# WHAT READERS SAY ABOUT
## SECOND CHANCE AT LOVE BOOKS

"I can't begin to thank you for the many, many hours of pure bliss I have received from the wonderful SECOND CHANCE [AT LOVE] books. Everyone I talk to lately has admitted their preference for SECOND CHANCE [AT LOVE] over all the other lines."
　　—*S. S., Phoenix, AZ**

"Hurrah for Berkley . . . the butterfly and its wonderful SECOND CHANCE AT LOVE."
　　—*G. B., Mount Prospect, IL**

"Thank you, thank you, thank you—I just had to write to let you know how much I love SECOND CHANCE AT LOVE . . ."
　　—*R. T., Abbeville, LA**

"It's so hard to wait 'til it's time for the next shipment . . . I hope your firm soon considers adding to the line."
　　—*P. D., Easton, PA**

"SECOND CHANCE AT LOVE is fantastic. I have been reading romances for as long as I can remember—and I enjoy SECOND CHANCE [AT LOVE] the best."
　　—*G. M., Quincy, IL**

*Names and addresses available upon request